Susan Gates was
a guitar player a
secondary school h
fiction – she rea
Cleethorpes public library. She also had a
all kinds of American literature, especially detective
stories, and went on to study American literature
at Warwick University. Then she became a teacher.
She taught in Malawi, Africa (she still has a scar
on her ankle from a mosquito bite that went septic),
and in County Durham, England. She has three
adorable teenage children (she has to say that – they
might read this book!): Laura, Alex and Chris.

Other books by Susan Gates

ATTACK OF THE TENTACLED TERROR
KILLER MUSHROOMS ATE MY GRAN

Susan Gates

Revenge of the Toffee Monster

PUFFIN BOOKS

PUFFIN BOOKS

Published by the Penguin Group
Penguin Books Ltd, 80 Strand, London WC2R 0RL, England
Penguin Putnam Inc., 375 Hudson Street, New York, New York 10014, USA
Penguin Books Australia Ltd, 250 Camberwell Road, Camberwell, Victoria 3124, Australia
Penguin Books Canada Ltd, 10 Alcorn Avenue, Toronto, Ontario, Canada M4V 3B2
Penguin Books India (P) Ltd, 11 Community Centre, Panchsheel Park, New Delhi – 110 017, India
Penguin Books (NZ) Ltd, Cnr Rosedale and Airborne Roads, Albany, Auckland, New Zealand
Penguin Books (South Africa) (Pty) Ltd, 24 Sturdee Avenue, Rosebank 2196, South Africa

Penguin Books Ltd, Registered Offices: 80 Strand, London WC2R 0RL, England

www.penguin.com

First published 1999
10

The moral right of the author has been asserted

Made and printed in England by Clays Ltd, St Ives plc

British Library Cataloguing in Publication Data
A CIP catalogue record for this book is available from the British Library

ISBN 0–141–30224–0

Chapter One

Lenny's bike skidded to a stop. He leapt off it and threw it on to the ground.

'What's this place?' he asked himself, out loud.

He read the name on a rusty metal sign. 'Butterworth's Toffee Works.'

'Where'd this place come from?' he demanded, as if it should have asked his permission to be there. It was just that he'd never spotted it before. This industrial estate was his territory. He was always riding his bike around it. He thought he knew every inch of it.

True, the Toffee Works was easy to miss. It was down an alleyway that was almost blocked with wheelie bins and stinking rubbish. It was a skinny building, squeezed in between two warehouses like the filling in a sandwich. It shouldn't be here, it didn't belong. It was made out of crumbling yellow brick. It looked as if there'd been some planning mistake. As if it had been left behind by accident when they'd bulldozed all the other old buildings to put up the modern factory units.

Lenny pushed aside a wheelie bin.

'What's this sign then?' he wondered. The other sign was a hand with a pointing finger. 'To the Toffee Museum. Free,' it said.

'I didn't know there was a Toffee Museum round here!' said Lenny. He sounded even more disapproving. He didn't like things happening on his territory that he didn't know about.

But he found himself thinking. 'Humm, might be worth a look.'

That showed how bored he was. Usually, if any of his friends had said, 'Hey, how about a look round the Toffee Museum?' he would have answered, 'Toffee Museum? You've got to be joking!'

But today, there were no friends around.

He'd called at everyone's house, even the kids he couldn't stand. And they were all on holiday. Every single one of them! It had been a nasty shock. He wasn't used to being on his own. He felt really strange. Like a lonesome seagull that's lost its flock. He was used to being in a big noisy gang of kids. He didn't know what to do with himself.

'They could've told me!' he grumbled. 'I didn't know they were all going away – at the same time!'

He still couldn't believe it. He felt angry and hurt. Like they'd got together and sneaked off behind his back. His mum and dad had no money for holidays. He'd nagged his mum. But she'd just got mad. 'Lenny,' she'd said. 'You'd better forget it. There's no way!'

And his new baby sister was no fun. She was still all floppy. Her mouth went square when she yelled her head off. And she was always yelling her head off. It gave Lenny a headache. He couldn't even read his comics in peace.

Once, he had tried to help. He had tried

to pick her up to comfort her. But Mum had come into the room. She had told him off. 'Give her to me, Lenny, you'll drop her! And look, your hands must be dirty. Her white Babygro is black now! I'll have to dress her all over again!'

Lenny frowned at the memory – it had made him feel so clumsy and stupid.

'My life is rubbish!' he muttered.

Times were bad. So bad that even a Toffee Museum seemed like a good way of killing time. Especially if it was free.

'Free!' said Lenny, reading the word out loud just to make sure.

Along with all his other troubles, like being abandoned by his friends and having a baby at home who wailed like a fire-engine, Lenny was stony broke. He'd just spent his last 35p on a Sparkle Bar. Now his pockets were as bare as his baby sister's bald head.

'You going into this museum place then, Lenny, my man?' Lenny asked himself.

'Might as well,' he answered back, with a shrug.

He'd been having a lot of conversations

with himself since he found out his friends had all sneaked away.

Another finger was pointing sternly to a little green door. 'This Way!' it said.

When Lenny went through the door he wheeled his bike with him. He thought bikes probably weren't allowed in Toffee Museums.

'But that's too bad! I'm not going to leave you outside to get nicked,' he muttered to his bike.

As soon as he got inside, he almost spun round and came out again.

'Whoops, big mistake, Lenny,' he told himself.

The Toffee Museum was not child-friendly. It was a gloomy room with dreary glass cases round the walls. There was dust everywhere. Dust in the cases – you could hardly see into them. Thick grey dust on the floor. There were no other footprints in the dust. No one had visited this Toffee Museum for a very long time.

'Not surprised,' thought Lenny, as he turned his bike round to go out. 'What a dump.'

Using the hem of his T-shirt, he rubbed at the dust on one of the cases. He made a little window. He leaned to peer into it. A face peered back at him.

'Aaagh! Whossat?'

He sprang back, his heart jumping about like a frog trapped in a bucket.

Very, very warily, he looked into the case again.

The face was still there, trapped under the glass. It stared spookily out at him. It was a chubby face, doughy and white with two sad black eyes. It had a sort of tartan cap on, on top of curly blond hair.

Lenny rubbed away some more of the dust.

'Phew!' he huffed a big sigh of relief. 'Lenny, you prat!' he told himself, pretending to wipe a waterfall of sweat off his brow. 'Don't wet your pants! It's only a picture – on an old toffee tin! And it's a girl!'

He could see now. The girl had old-fashioned clothes on, a white lacy frock with lacy knee-length knickers underneath it and black button-up boots. She was pulling a toy horse on wheels. It was made of wood

6

with stick legs and a barrel-shaped body. It wasn't a cute toy horse. It had a mean flat little head, like a snake.

The toffee tin was the biggest tin Lenny had ever seen. It was about a metre long. And above the little girl's head it said: 'Butterworth's Superior Toffee. By appointment to Queen Victoria.'

Lenny shivered. He felt uneasy, even a little scared. But he didn't know why. He wheeled his bike along to another case. It had dead bluebottle flies in it and bits of cracked yellow newspaper with articles about Butterworth's toffee being the best and winning lots of prizes. There was a dusty silver cup and some faded rosettes. Nothing to be scared of there. But all the time, he could feel the eyes of that little girl on the toffee tin tracking him round the room, as if she wanted to ask him something. He shivered again. He almost yelled out, 'What do you want?' but stopped himself, just in time. He decided she was a pain in the neck.

'Bet she was a real misery guts,' he thought.

Then, all of a sudden, he felt heavy with sadness. For no reason! It was like a rock in his stomach. It swept over him in a deep, black wave. He slumped down beside his bike. He felt almost too weak to move, as if all the energy had been drained from his body.

'Got to get back outside,' he told himself. It was so dreary and airless in here. All this dusty, sad, forgotten stuff. It belonged to history, to a hundred years ago, not to nowadays.

And it was so quiet. Everything about this place seemed dead. It was like a ghost museum. Even the flies were ancient, as dried-up and shrivelled as mummies!

'Get out of this dump,' Lenny told himself urgently. 'Get some fresh air!' He lurched to his feet. He started wheeling his bike quickly towards the door, looking over his shoulder, as if he was running away from something.

Then, suddenly, he stopped. His nose wrinkled up.

'What's that smell?'

It wasn't the musty, dusty smell of the Toffee Museum. It was a new, fresh smell

8

– a wonderful, tempting, delicious smell, like warm sugary doughnuts. Lenny forgot he'd been desperate to escape. He forgot about going outside. He stopped and sniffed again.

'Mmmmmm,' he was thinking, his nose quivering like a tracker dog's.

A smile broke out, very slowly, on his face. He loved that smell. He recognized it, from the time his mum had made toffee apples at Hallowe'en. This place wasn't as dead as he'd thought. Someone must be alive somewhere. Someone was in the Toffee Works right now. And they were making Butterworth's toffee.

'See that other door over there?' Lenny asked his bike. 'Wonder where it leads to?'

He wasn't scared now. Just breathing in that sweet, buttery, hot-caramel smell made all his fears float away. He could follow it for miles!

'Let's go and find where it comes from,' said Lenny.

He forgot about the creepy child on the toffee tin. He just wanted to follow that smell. But, as he wheeled his bike out of the Toffee Museum, the sad eyes in the glass case were watching him, every step of the way.

Chapter Two

Lenny and his bike followed the delicious smell. It lured them on. It led them along a dark passage, down three steps, along another passage into the heart of the Toffee Works.

'This is it!' said Lenny, sniffing hard. 'I think it's coming from behind this door!'

He pushed the door open. And he was staring into a vast kitchen. At first he was dazzled by white tiled walls, glinting copper pans. It was so clean and bright in here after the gloomy toffee museum that it almost blinded him.

'Wow,' he said to himself in a stunned whisper.

He had to blink and blink again until his eyes got used to it. He saw big black stoves and scrubbed snowy-white wooden tables. Then a movement caught his eye.

'There's somebody here!' he hissed to his bike. 'Over there!'

Someone stood at the far end of the kitchen, among the gleaming copper pans. She had her back to him. She had a white coat on, like a doctor. Her skinny legs were in green rubber boots. Her white hat had a bright orange hair-net billowing out from beneath it.

It seemed like a very strange outfit. But Lenny was reassured by it: 'My Granny Wang wore clothes like that when she was a banana pie maker in that factory,' he reminded himself.

Granny Wang used to work a machine. It squirted banana cream into pies as they joggled along a conveyor belt. But this toffee maker didn't need a machine. She was using her hands. Using them to do conjuring tricks with toffee!

Lenny watched her, his mouth a round 'O' of wonder. It all happened so fast. First, she greased her hands. She grabbed a lump of soft toffee out of a pan. It was golden and clear like amber. She threw the toffee at a hook on the wall. It stuck. Then she strode quickly backwards, pulling toffee out from the hook into three glistening ropes that stretched like elastic as she walked.

Lenny held his breath. 'It's gonna break,' he thought. 'It's gonna come unstuck from that hook!'

But, amazingly, it didn't break. It didn't fall off the hook. That toffee just carried on stretching. She tugged it out into long, golden ropes the whole length of the kitchen. It would be as thin as spaghetti soon!

She almost backed into Lenny.

'Sorry!' he said.

But she didn't see or hear him. She was concentrating too hard. In the whole world, nothing existed except her, and the toffee.

And what she did next needed total attention. Lenny couldn't believe his eyes. She started to twirl those toffee ropes, all three of them. Faster, faster they went, like skipping ropes in the playground. They looped round again and again. But they didn't snap, they didn't even get tangled. It was like magic!

The kitchen seemed filled with whirling golden rainbows. Soon they were spinning so fast they were just a blur. It made Lenny dizzy just watching.

'That's beautiful,' he thought, his eyes wide with wonder. 'That's class.'

The toffee maker stood sturdy in her green rubber boots, so close he could have reached out and touched her. But he wouldn't have risked it. It would be like waking her from a dream. She seemed hypnotized by the twirling toffee. She was still as a stone statue. Only her wrists moved, expertly flicking the toffee round and round, round and round.

'What's she going to do now?' thought Lenny, dazzled by her skill.

She'd started to swap the toffee from hand to hand. Criss, cross, criss, cross, like a cat's cradle. Her quick fingers flickered like birds in a bush. She was working with lightning speed now. The ropes plaited themselves, starting from the hook end, until the glittering rainbows vanished and all that was left was one fat toffee plait that stretched right across the room.

'Cor!' muttered Lenny, deeply impressed. 'That's really clever. That's –' He was lost for words – something that almost never happened to him.

But she wasn't finished yet. Whop! With one deft heave the toffee maker slung the plait on to a long bench. She took a silver knife out of her pocket. She worked her way quickly along the bench in a frenzy of slashing. Chop, chop, chop, chop. The plait fell apart into lots of short, twisted candy sticks.

And Lenny just knew, if you measured them, that each of those candy sticks would be *exactly* the same length.

She'd finished her work. The toffee maker rested now, with her pointy elbows on the long bench. It was hard work, keeping all that wild, whippy toffee under control. Sometimes it seemed to have a life of its own.

Lenny started to clap. He just couldn't help himself. That toffee juggling display! He'd never seen anything like it! His eyes were still dazed by golden rainbows.

'Yay!' he cheered, punching the air with

his fist. 'Are you a magician or something, Mrs Woman? Are you famous or something? You should be on the telly!'

The toffee maker looked up. She noticed him for the first time. She seemed to Lenny to be extremely ancient. She had a pinched little tortoise face and wispy white hair that poked through her orange hair-net. But she had bright little eyes, as sharp and green as lime-drops. She didn't look thrilled to see him.

'What are you doing?' she asked him, in a rusty voice that sounded as if it wasn't used much. 'I don't allow children in my Toffee Works. They're unhygienic.'

Lenny wasn't listening. His teachers were always writing that on his reports. 'This boy does not listen!' Instead he was hopping about, mad with impatience.

'Can you teach me to twirl toffee like that, Mrs Woman?'

He had a sudden, marvellous vision of himself on a stage, twirling toffee while the audience gasped in admiration. 'Bravo!' they would cry. 'More! More!' Lenny had no idea what he was going to be when he grew up. It worried him quite a bit. But now he knew what he wanted to be. He'd discovered the perfect career. He wanted to spend his whole life being a toffee twirler.

'I want to do that toffee twirling thing!' insisted Lenny. 'I can do that!'

The toffee maker didn't smile at his frantic enthusiasm. Instead she pursed up her lips as if she was sucking an acid drop.

'Let's get one or two things straight,' she said, in her old, cracked voice. 'Firstly, I am not Mrs Woman. My name is Miss Butterworth. And secondly, the correct name is toffee throwing. Not toffee twirling.'

'Yeah, but can anyone do it?'

Miss Butterworth's cold, lime-drop eyes looked deadly serious. Even Lenny stopped leaping about and listened.

She held up her greasy palms. 'It's dangerous work,' she said. 'The toffee is like hot glue. Can you work so fast that it doesn't stick and your skin doesn't burn and blister? Can you work so fast that it doesn't set? Are you from four generations of toffee makers, like I am?'

Lenny's face was tragic with disappointment. 'My mum's Chinese,' he said. 'Does that mean I can't throw toffee?'

'Doesn't matter where your mum's from,' said Miss Butterworth in her sour voice. 'Or your dad. Cricklewood, China, Outer Mongolia, Africa. Doesn't matter. It's being a Butterworth that matters. I am the last Butterworth. Toffee is in my blood.'

'Oh,' said Lenny, crushed. 'I just wanted to do it,' he told her, with desperate longing in his voice. 'All them toffee ropes whizzing about. All golden and bright. It was like a laser display or something! That toffee twirling is a really class act!'

'Toffee throwing,' corrected Miss Butterworth sternly.

She was going to say more harsh things. She didn't like children much. They got on her nerves. But she took a second, curious look at this one. She couldn't entirely dislike a child who was such a big fan of toffee throwing.

She saw a shrimpy little kid in front of her. He wore black baggy pants and a baggy T-shirt and a black woolly hat pulled right down to his eyebrows, even though it was summer. He was wheeling a red bike that seemed far too big for him.

'How did you get in here?' she challenged him, in a voice that was not quite so chilly.

'I came to look at the Toffee Museum,' Lenny told her.

For a second or two Miss Butterworth looked blank, as if she'd entirely forgotten the Toffee Museum existed.

'It's a dump,' said Lenny. He was feeling bitterly disappointed. His future as a world-famous toffee thrower had just been snatched away from him.

'Yes, well,' Miss Butterworth snapped. 'This whole place is going down the drain. And it's your fault!'

'Me?' protested Lenny, looking wide-eyed and innocent. He always used this expression when he was blamed for anything, even if he was panicking underneath. 'I didn't do nothing! I never even knew this place existed! Why is it my fault?'

'Because boys like you,' said Miss Butterworth accusingly, 'used to love our toffee. Once, every boy had a fluffy lump of

Butterworth's Superior Toffee in his blazer pocket. They were never without it! Especially our prize-winning treacle toffee. But do you buy it now? Do you? Do you?' demanded Miss Butterworth, her tortoise head wobbling and her green eyes flashing. 'No, you flipping well don't!'

Lenny thought guiltily of the Sparkle Bar in his pocket. He decided he'd better keep quiet about that.

'So we're going bust!' ranted Miss Butterworth, waggling her greasy finger at him. 'Soon Butterworth's Toffee Works will be finished. Finito! We only sell our toffee to the Bideawee Old Folks' Home now. And they're always complaining that it glues their false teeth together. You children used to be our main market. I don't know what's gone wrong. I don't understand children today!'

Lenny said, cautiously, 'Do you get out much, Miss Butterworth?'

'I've barely been outside this Toffee Works in fifty years! This Toffee Works is my life. I've got toffee in my –'

'Yes, yes, I know,' said Lenny soothingly.

'You've got toffee in your blood.' He was bursting to speak now. He felt he had something important to contribute. Miss Butterworth might be a toffee expert. But he, Lenny, was an expert on all kinds of modern-day sweets.

He whipped the Sparkle Bar out of his pocket.

'What's that?' demanded Miss Butterworth, scowling.

'It's what all the kids are buying today, instead of your toffee.'

Miss Butterworth inspected the Sparkle Bar as if it was some kind of strange, exotic animal.

Then she sniffed in disgust. 'I can't see the attraction, I'm sure. If I was a child and I had the choice between *that* and a nice, sticky lump of Butterworth's prize-winning treacle toffee, I know which one I'd choose! Especially as our treacle toffee is great for mending punctures on your bike.'

Lenny sighed. He knew it was going to be an uphill struggle – explaining Sparkle Bars to someone who'd missed out on fifty years of sweet manufacture.

He decided he had to be brutal. 'Look, Missis,' he said.

'Miss!'

'Look,' Lenny rushed on, 'Butterworth's toffee isn't fun, is it? I mean, it's so kind of . . . old-fashioned! It isn't cool! It's about as cool as, well, cold Brussels sprouts!'

'What do you mean!' Miss Butterworth was outraged. 'Toffee isn't supposed to be fun, young man! Toffee is a very serious business!'

Lenny gave an even deeper sigh. He was talking to a toffee freak here. Someone who couldn't understand why everyone wasn't nuts about toffee. Someone who just wouldn't admit that Butterworth's toffee had a major image problem.

He tried again. 'Look, when you buy this Butterworth's Superior Toffee, all you get is the toffee. Right?'

'Of course,' said Miss Butterworth, looking baffled. 'Except if you buy twenty-five trays of our brazil nut toffee we might, only *might*, mind, give you a free toffee hammer.'

'A free toffee hammer!' Lenny raised his eyebrows. 'Look, with Sparkle Bars you get loads of extras. Loads of *fun* extras. See this great wrapper for a start!' Lenny held up the Sparkle Bar so its silver wrapper flashed in the light. 'This wrapper is neon, it lights up in the dark!'

'Why?' asked Miss Butterworth in her brisk, no-nonsense voice.

'Why?' said Lenny. It was his turn to be baffled. 'I don't know why! It's just cool, isn't it? And you get free things called Sparklets inside. That's these little glittery disc things that you can play games with and collect in an album because they've got pictures of monsters on. And –' Lenny had to pause for breath. He was fired up now, getting really carried away. '*And* there's a number inside the wrapper and if you get the lucky number you get the chance to go to Disney-World® and there's tokens on the wrapper and if you cut *them* out and collect 133 of them you get a free Sparkle backpack *and* –'

'What's in it?' asked Miss Butterworth suddenly.

'Eh?' said Lenny, surprised at such an odd question. 'What do you mean, what's in it?'

'What's this Sparkle Bar made of? Our toffee is only made from the purest ingredients.'

'I don't know,' shrugged Lenny, annoyed at being interrupted. He squinted at the wrapper. The ingredients were listed in tiny print but he didn't recognize any of them. 'It's got these numbers with E in front of them and some other long chemical names I can't pronounce. But anyway, when you eat a Sparkle Bar if fizzes blue foam and turns your teeth bright blue!'

'That's terrible!'

'No, it's *supposed* to! Because it's good fun, isn't it? And there's a great advert for them on telly. There's this alien with green tentacles. Right? And he's on this purple planet, right, and he's eating a Sparkle Bar! And he's saying, in this sort of alien voice, 'WOW! You earthlings certainly know a thing or two about candy!' And there's this song in the background. Every kid knows the Sparkle Bar song! We sing it all the time!'

Lenny took a great lungful of air. He exploded into song. Miss Butterworth

looked on, her expression becoming more
and more pained.

'*WOW! Cosmic kids eat Sparkle Bars!*
WOW! Sparkle Bars are ace!
They WOW the world, the universe!
They WOW aliens in space!'

'Have you finished yet?' said Miss Butterworth, raking a finger round in her ear. 'I
think I've gone deaf!'

'Sorry!' But you're supposed to sing it
really loud.'

'So, let me get this right – you're saying
that all this fizzing and glowing in the dark
and free gifts and silly songs makes these
Sparkle Bars more attractive to children?'

'Course it does!' cried Lenny. 'That's
what I've been trying to tell you! It's fun,
isn't it? It makes you feel good! And every-
body's heard of Sparkle Bars. Kids love 'em.
Kids buy 'em all the time! Nobody's heard
of Butterworth's Toffee. No kids I know
have ever heard of it!'

'We did advertise once,' mused Miss
Butterworth, 'back in my grandfather's

time.' Her face screwed up as if she was trying hard to remember the details.

'We had an advertisement in *Toffee Times*. It said at the top in big, bold letters, "SILENCE THAT NOISY CHILD!" And there was a picture as well. It showed three children, struggling to speak. But they couldn't, because their jaws were stuck together with toffee. And their parents were looking really pleased and saying: "Ah peace at last! Thanks to Butterworth's prize-winning treacle toffee, the parents' friend!"'

'NO, NO, NO, NO, NO!' yelled Lenny, almost leaping up and down with frustration. 'That's wrong! Everything about it is totally wrong! That's about keep-ing kids quiet. Kids don't like that these days! Take me, for example. I'm a noisy kid –'

'I noticed,' murmured Miss Butterworth, whose ears were still ringing from the Sparkle Bar song.

'But I like being noisy! I don't like being told to keep quiet. No, no, no, no, no!' said Lenny again, shaking his head hopelessly. 'You just don't understand. You don't understand anything! You need someone to tell you what modern kids like!'

And then, ping! he had a brilliant brain-wave. It glittered in his mind like a million Sparkle Bar wrappers.

'I'll tell you what, if you like!' said Lenny, in his chirpiest voice. 'I could be a sort of – consultant. I could tell you how to make kids buy Butterworth's toffee. I'd be dead good at that. I'm a typical, ordinary, average kid! I'm just the person you need!'

Actually, in his heart of hearts, he thought nothing would make kids buy Butterworth's toffee. He thought Butterworth's toffee was doomed. But he was broke. And bored to death without his friends. And being a toffee consultant seemed like the perfect way to pass the time.

'I won't charge much,' he assured her, brightly.

Miss Butterworth's green eyes narrowed suspiciously when he mentioned money. But she didn't instantly turn down his offer.

So naturally Lenny thought, 'Great, I've got the job!'

He had plenty of advice to give her.

Loads and loads of it. He hardly knew where to start. 'That toffee throwing,' he began. 'Now that's really exciting. That's brilliant, that is! But then what do you do with the toffee? You put it into those horrible old-fashioned tins.' He broke off for a moment. The feelings of dreariness and melancholy he'd felt in the Toffee Museum seemed to swamp him all over again. He shook them off and ploughed on. 'That tin with that girl on it. That creepy girl in that lacy frock with that wooden horse thing. She looks so *miserable*. She doesn't make you feel good at all.'

Miss Butterworth looked puzzled. She didn't seem to know what he was talking about.

'You know,' prompted Lenny, 'that massive great big tin in the Toffee Museum?'

'Oh, that tin!' said Miss Butterworth, nodding proudly. 'That tin is part of our toffee history. It was made to celebrate Queen Victoria's Golden Jubilee in 1887. But,' she added, 'you've got it wrong. That's not a girl on the tin. That's a boy. His name was Harold.'

Lenny stared at her, his eyes goggling. 'Come on!' he said. 'You're kidding me! That's a girl! I know what a girl looks like! She's got a frock on! And a hat with ribbons.'

'That's young Master Harold, of course,' corrected Miss Butterworth, as if she couldn't understand why anyone would make such a foolish mistake. 'In his Scottish bonnet. Little Victorian boys wore dresses like that – until they were three or four, that is. Then they got their curls cut off and their first set of proper boy's trousers.'

'Wha–at?' Lenny spluttered, choking with indignation. 'Poor kid! No wonder he looks fed up! I'd be *really* fed up if I was on a toffee tin dressed like that. For everyone to laugh at!'

The very thought made him squirm with embarrassment.

At first he'd decided to hate the spooky child on the toffee tin. But now he'd totally changed his mind. Lenny was on his side. His heart was almost bursting with pity for him. No wonder the poor kid looked miserable. He'd got plenty to be miserable about!

'It's a disgrace!' raved Lenny. 'No one should do that to a kid! It's child cruelty!'

'You've got it all wrong again,' said Miss Butterworth calmly. 'No one would laugh at young Master Harold. I told you, all little boys wore skirts then. Folks would just think, "Awww! What a sweet angelic child!" The ideal child to advertise Butterworth's Superior Toffee.'

'Sweet!' Lenny spat the word out, as if it were poison. 'Angelic! Poor kid!' He thought of young Harold's eyes, staring at him from the glass case. Those strange, haunted eyes, full of desperate sadness. It made him feel really upset.

'Why does he look so sad then?' Lenny appealed to Miss Butterworth, 'Do you know why? Did you know him?'

Miss Butterworth shook her head. 'I never met him,' she said, her hard, lime-drop eyes softening a little. 'But I know all about him. Poor Master Harold is part of our toffee history. Our secret history. A very tragic part. And he came to a very sticky end.'

Lenny forgot there was a world outside.

He forgot he had to be home for his tea. Time had no meaning in the Toffee Works. It felt like he'd been here for ever.

'Tell me what happened to young Master Harold,' Lenny begged Miss Butterworth. 'I just got to know.'

Miss Butterworth didn't reply immediately. She seemed to be thinking it over.

'Please,' said Lenny. The tragic child on the toffee tin had touched his heart. Lenny instinctively felt, although he didn't have the details yet, that his life had been rubbish.

Miss Butterworth was still pondering. She had no family left. She was the last Butterworth. She was eighty-four and soon she would be dead like all the others. Harold's story should die with her. She had never spoken about it to anyone. Why speak now, especially to a child?

But, she reminded herself, this child was not just any child. He appreciated toffee throwing. He had pleaded with her to teach him. And his Mum was Chinese. Wasn't toffee first discovered in ancient China? Weren't there ancient recipes for toffee apples in old Chinese manuscripts?

Perhaps, even though he was not a Butterworth, this boy had toffee in his blood.

'I've decided to tell you,' she said, finally, as if she was granting him a big favour. 'I'm going to show you the Butterworth's private museum, the one the public never see. Leave your bike there.'

Lenny's bike was his most precious possession. He felt anxious when it was out of his sight.

But the glinting copper pans almost blinded him. The boiling toffee smelt so syrupy-sweet it made his head swim. 'Are you coming or not?' Miss Butterworth asked him sharply, stumping ahead of him in her green rubber boots and white toffee-making outfit.

Lenny nodded. He propped his bike against the wall and left it. Just like that, with not even a backward glance. And he followed Miss Butterworth, into the heart of the Toffee Works.

Chapter Three

They were climbing up twisty stairs. Lenny didn't know where she was leading him. But with every step they got further away from the world outside and deeper into the Toffee Works.

'Here we are,' Miss Butterworth panted. She pushed open a door.

They were in a sort of tower room. Cobwebs hung down like ragged banners. The roof was a huge glass dome. But it was so grimy and crusted with bird droppings that only murky light came through it.

'Wow,' marvelled Lenny, peering into the gloom. 'Where is this? You can't see this from the street!'

'We're at the top of the Toffee Works,' said Miss Butterworth. 'In my grandad

Josiah Butterworth's laboratory. He spent all his time up here. This is where he did his experiments.'

Lenny could see glass flasks and pipes and rubber tubes lying in dusty heaps on benches.

'What's that?' he was going to ask. Over there, in the shadows, was a great hulking shape covered by a sheet. But before he could get the question out of his mouth, something else caught his attention.

It was poor little Harold's wooden horse – or what was left of it. It was lying on its side, in the dust. One of its wheels was missing, one of its stick legs was snapped. And its mean snaky head was hanging from its body.

Just seeing it gave Lenny a terrible shock. It made Harold seem like a real person, not just a boy on a toffee tin. Lenny glanced quickly round, as if he half-expected a pasty face and two mournful eyes to be watching him from under a bench. But nothing moved. Nothing disturbed the dust.

He crouched beside the horse, stroking its wooden back. Touching Harold's broken toy made Lenny feel deeply, desperately sad . . .

Then he saw what Miss Butterworth was taking out of a tall, thin cupboard. 'Hey, that's Harold's frock, isn't it?' said Lenny, excitedly. 'That's his cap and his boots!'

Miss Butterworth wiped some dust away and spread Harold's outfit out on a bench. First his cap, then his frock and his boots. It looked so eerie, it made Lenny shiver. As if the clothes might suddenly get up and walk around on their own.

'This is just one of his frocks,' corrected Miss Butterworth. 'In some ways Harold was a very lucky boy. He had plenty of clothes and toys. Those were the days,' said Miss Butterworth, shaking her head, 'when Butterworth's toffee was a really big name! Everyone ate it, including the Queen of the Realm!'

'Wait a minute,' said Lenny, 'was this Harold a giant child then? You said Victorian kids wore clothes like this until they were three or four. I could nearly fit in this dress! I know I'm small for my age but Harold must have been humungous!'

'Ahhh,' said Miss Butterworth, pensively. Her face clouded over. Her sharp little eyes seemed troubled. 'He probably wore those baby clothes longer than most Victorian boys. He was six or seven when he sat for that portrait on the toffee tin.'

'Six or seven!' roared Lenny. He felt more on Harold's side than ever. He was practically frothing at the mouth with outrage. 'That's criminal, that is! That's child cruelty!'

'I don't think his parents were being cruel,' declared Miss Butterworth, stiffly. 'I mean, not deliberately. I just don't think they noticed.'

'Didn't notice!' spluttered Lenny. 'My mum and dad would notice if I was walking round dressed like that! My friends at school would notice! You bet they would!'

'Harold didn't go to school,' said Miss Butterworth. 'And his parents were always busy. His father, that's Josiah Butterworth, my grandad, spent all his time up here, in this laboratory, doing toffee experiments. Toffee was his life. It was all he thought about. And Harold's mother was a great beauty. She was very posh! She loved fine dresses and jewellery. She was always going out visiting and going to balls. She didn't have time for Harold either. I don't think she found him a very attractive child. So, I suppose Harold was a bit neglected –'

'What happened to him then?' said Lenny, impatiently. 'Poor kid, I feel really sorry for him. His life was rubbish!'

Miss Butterworth hesitated. She'd surprised herself by giving this much away. The secret history of the Butterworths was sinister and dark. It was better kept hidden. Yet, here she was, telling it all to this modern child who'd just cycled in off the streets.

Why was she doing it? Miss Butterworth was crabby and tough as old boots. In most things she couldn't be fooled. But when it came to toffee she was like a different person. She got carried away. She let her heart rule her head.

'Perhaps this child was meant to come here,' she persuaded herself. 'What if he's our guardian angel? What if he *can* save my Toffee Works? What if he can make Butterworth's prize-winning treacle toffee popular with children again?' It was the only thing left in the world she really cared about.

She peered closely at Lenny, inspecting him. He'd taken his woolly hat off to give his head a good scratch. He didn't look much like an angel. Angels don't usually turn up on red bikes. 'But guardian angels come in all shapes and sizes,' Miss Butterworth reminded herself.

Of course, Lenny had no idea that Miss Butterworth saw him as some kind of toffee saviour. If he'd known, he would have been really alarmed.

'What happened to poor little Harold?' repeated Lenny, scratching his hedgehog hair. 'You said he came to a sticky end. Tell me quick. What happened?'

He felt personally involved with Harold now, as if Harold was his best friend or his brother.

Miss Butterworth smiled at Lenny's interest. It made her even more sure that, in some mysterious way, he was heaven-sent. It was a creaky, grim little smile. Lenny thought, 'Why's she twisting her mouth up like that?' But those smile muscles hadn't been used for a long, long time.

'My grandfather Josiah Butterworth was a very brainy chap,' continued Miss Butterworth. 'He was interested in all sorts of things. In biology, for instance – he dissected frogs up here. He kept them in a bucket.'

'Ugh, gross!' said Lenny, wrinkling his nose.

'Ah, yes,' said Miss Butterworth fondly. 'They used to escape. There were frogs hopping about all over the place.'

Lenny looked round, shuddering. Then he remembered that she was talking about a long time ago. More than a hundred years. So why did it seem so real to him, as if it had happened yesterday?

'He was always inventing new and secret recipes for toffee,' said Miss Butterworth, warming to her subject. 'He was fascinated by machinery and by electricity. Of course electricity was a brand-new invention then. He had a vision! He wanted Butterworth's Toffee Works to be the most modern in the world, filled with machines, all worked by electricity! This,' she said moving quickly across the tower room and whipping off the sheet, 'is the humbug machine he invented.'

'Wow!' said Lenny. 'Look at that beast!'

The machine looked like a massive iron monster. It was covered in dials and gauges. Coils of wire sprouted from it, thick as your wrist.

'Did it really work?' asked Lenny.

'Why yes! It made an almighty racket and shook the floor but it worked all right. The lumps of toffee mixture went along this conveyor belt here. Then these,' Miss Butterworth pointed to a forest of metal paddles, big as tennis racquets, 'slapped them into a humbug shape. Then this,' she showed him something like a gigantic fish slice, 'flicked them into the tins. Apparently it was quite a sight when it was working, with those paddles whacking away like mad. Folks came from miles around to see it.'

'Does it work now?' asked Lenny, who longed to see all the paddles whacking.

'Oh no, not now. It's never been used since that dreadful night when poor little Harold ... But hang on,' said Miss Butterworth, 'I'm getting ahead of myself here! First I've got to tell you how one of Josiah Butterworth's toffee inventions went tragically wrong.'

Above their heads the cobwebs rustled. They were spiky with flies' legs and wings. Where did that cold gust of wind come from? It made the ribbons on Harold's cap flutter. Lenny looked nervously round. But there was no one in the tower room with them.

'Are you listening?' said Miss Butterworth sternly. He might be a guardian angel but he still needed telling. Even angels had to pay attention. And she was getting to the really important bit.

'One night,' said Miss Butterworth, her voice slow and dripping with doom, 'Josiah Butterworth created a living creature, made entirely out of brazil nut toffee.'

'Come on!' said Lenny. 'You're joking!' He meant to laugh: 'Ha, ha ha!' But somehow it came out as a nervous giggle.

'I *never* make jokes about toffee, young man!' declared Miss Butterworth, indignantly. She thought toffee was such marvellous stuff that it could be used for almost anything, including creating life. But even she had to admit, 'Well, Josiah *might* have added one or two secret ingredients.'

'You mean you're serious?' gasped Lenny. 'Where did he do it? Where did he create this living creature?'

'In this very room,' said Miss Butterworth, in a low and ghostly voice.

Lenny could feel the skin at the back of his neck crawl. He wriggled his shoulders to try and stop it.

'He was working late,' said Miss Butterworth. 'It was almost midnight. And there was a storm. They say it was the worst storm in living memory! Crashing thunder, great jagged forks of lightning. But Josiah didn't notice such things. He didn't even notice if it was day or night when he was busy with his frogs and his toffee and all his other experiments. On this particular night all his toffee machines were switched on. All humming away, flashing like traffic lights. This room was crackling with electricity! Massive voltages! Remember, people weren't used to electricity then – they didn't know how dangerous it could be. There was a huge copper vat of brazil nut toffee – over there!'

Miss Butterworth's arm flew out as she pointed into the darkness. Lenny's head whipped round. But there was nothing to see except trembling shadows.

'They say the vat was so big you could get a horse in it! Josiah never did things by halves! It had thick wires leading into it to heat up the toffee and to work a gigantic metal whisk that stirred it round and round. So it was humming along nicely, heating up and whisking . . . when things went terribly wrong. No one knew what really happened. All Josiah remembered was a hissing sound and thick black smoke and a smell like bonfires. Then he fell to the floor with his hair on end, stiff as a kipper. They think a great lightning bolt came through the glass roof. It struck the big copper vat of brazil nut toffee, a direct hit, and bingo, there was a gigantic bang – it was heard several streets away and the whole tower room lit up with blue flashes that could be seen right across the river!'

'This Toffee Creature –' said Lenny, in

a quavering voice. He couldn't finish his sentence.

'Just wait! I'm coming to that! – So when my grandad Josiah Butterworth woke up, the vat was a smoking ruin. But out of it was climbing this creature, this living thing –'

'He must have nearly died of fright!' gasped Lenny. 'He must have wet himself!'

'He did not!' said Miss Butterworth. 'He was thrilled to bits! He jumped around with joy! He greeted the creature! He rushed to hug it but, of course, it was too sticky. "My creation!" he cried. "My wonderful Toffee Creature!"'

'So did he make it deliberately then?' asked Lenny, his eyes boggling. 'Or was it an accident?'

'Who knows?' said Miss Butterworth, flinging her arms wide. 'Who knows what was in Josiah's mind? He was a toffee genius! He always knew, as I do, that toffee is a miraculous substance. That it has limitless possibilities! And when he was a boy his hero was Dr Frankenstein. But who knows? Whether he did it deliberately or not, his Toffee Creature was born.'

'Where was Harold when all this was going on?'

'He was asleep in bed in Butterworth Towers, just next door to the Toffee Works. Anyhow, Josiah was so excited by what he'd created that he went rushing to wake Harold up. He brought him back to this room to see the incredible creature.'

'Don't tell me Harold wasn't scared stiff!'

'He was at first. But remember, poor little Harold was a lonely and neglected boy. He had no friends. Even his mum and dad ignored him. So after a time, he and the Toffee Creature became constant companions. The creature followed him round like a dog –'

'What did it look like?' asked Lenny, more excited now than scared. 'I can't imagine what a Toffee Creature would look like!'

'It was very strange,' mused Miss Butterworth. 'Of course, I didn't see it myself. I only know about this from family stories. But they say it looked very lumpy and warty. You'd expect that, I suppose, because it was made of brazil nut toffee. In some ways it looked like a great grizzly bear – a bear made out of toffee, of course. But in other ways it looked very frog-like. It had rather goggly eyes and a big stretchy mouth and webbed feet and hands and these springy back legs –'

'Did it talk? What did it say?'

'It couldn't talk. You can't expect miracles! It was a very crude life form. They say it made some sort of croaking sound when it was upset. And it wasn't very brainy, poor thing. In fact, it was thick as two short planks. It could only be taught one command: "Fetch!" It loved fetching things for people. Slippers, pipes, Harold's little horse. Anything it thought they needed. It only wanted to be helpful. It wanted people to say "Good Toffee Creature" and pat it on the head. But of course they never did because everything it fetched was ruined.'

'Was that because it was all sticky?'

'That's right.' Miss Butterworth shook her head and sighed. 'It was a warm-blooded creature so obviously the toffee never really set properly. You couldn't pat it on the head, even if you'd wanted to, because your hand would have stuck. As a life form it was a total disaster. It caused commotion wherever it went. Of course it couldn't go far. It had to be hidden at Butterworth Towers. It couldn't be taken out in public. Imagine it looming up out of a London fog! There would have been mass panic! In the end, even keeping it in the house was impossible.'

Lenny imagined the sticky Toffee Creature lumbering around his own living-room, desperately trying to be helpful. It would drive his mum bananas! 'Put that down!' his mum would say. 'Don't touch those Babygros. You've got sticky finger-marks everywhere!' If the Toffee Creature tried to fetch you something, say your football magazine, you'd have to rip it off its hands like Velcro! And then it would be torn to shreds and the pages would all stick together. And what if it tried to pick up his new baby sister to stop her crying? Lenny cringed at the thought . . .

'I bet it was always getting told off,' said Lenny, glumly. 'I bet it was always in trouble!'

'It was,' agreed Miss Butterworth. 'It couldn't do anything right. The servants hated it because it made more work for them. They had to clean up wherever it went. Harold's mother called it a hideous creature. It was banished to the Toffee Works where it made a kind of nest in the burnt-out vat it was born in. Even its master, Josiah, lost interest in it when he found out it wasn't very bright. I think he was secretly hoping his creation would be a genius, like him.'

'That's terrible,' said Lenny. 'You seen those stickers in cars, "A dog is for life and not just for Christmas"? Josiah shouldn't have made it, should he, if he didn't want to look after it? I mean, a Toffee Creature is for life, isn't it, even if it does try to pick up your baby sister!'

Miss Butterworth looked utterly baffled at Lenny's outburst. But she went on. 'Not everyone hated the Toffee Creature. Not everyone insulted it and drove it away. Harold saw past the stickiness and the wartiness and the mess. He saw it was a gentle, timid creature who only wanted some kindness. He and Clum –'

'Clum?' interrupted Lenny. 'Who's Clum?'

'Ah,' said Miss Butterworth, 'I forgot to tell you. Everyone was always saying, "Go away, you clumsy creature!" and "How clumsy you are!" to the Toffee Creature. So naturally it thought its name was Clumsy. Harold didn't like that name – so he shortened it to Clum and –'

'My Granny Wang had a dog who thought its name was "Down boy!" Lenny burst in. 'So what happened then? Did Harold and Clum become best friends?'

'I was going to tell you,' said Miss Butterworth, 'before you rudely interrupted.'

'Sorry,' said Lenny, smacking a hand over his mouth to make himself shut up.

'Harold and Clum were a pair, like eggs and bacon, cheese and pickle. They were inseparable! Clum thought he was a Butterworth too. Harold used to lead him round the Toffee Works – not by the hand, of course, because they would have stuck together.'

Lenny's hand was still resting on Harold's broken toy horse. Almost without thinking, he stroked its wooden head. And suddenly an amazing picture flashed into his mind. Of Harold and Clum here in this very room. He could see them now. Harold, that chubby, serious child in his lacy frock and button-up boots, pulling his little toy horse. And shambling behind him, Clum the Toffee Creature, with his great, big froggy head and goggly eyes gazing adoringly at little Harold, his best and only friend.

Lenny forgot he'd promised not to interrupt. 'Where's the toffee vat Clum lived in?' he said looking around the tower room. He couldn't see it. Perhaps it was hidden away behind the massive humbug machine.

'I don't know,' said Miss Butterworth. 'It was taken away long ago.'

Lenny looked disappointed. Harold's things were here, in the Butterworth's private museum. His clothes were here and his toys. But there was nothing here, nothing that he could look at or touch, that would make Clum seem as real to him as poor little Harold did.

'Isn't there anything left of Clum?'

'What do you mean?' demanded Miss

Butterworth, flashing him a suspicious look. For a moment Lenny thought that she looked scared. But no, he must have been mistaken. Miss Butterworth was like a fierce, snappy little terrier. She wasn't afraid of anything.

'I mean, like a picture of him or something?' said Lenny. 'Anything to remind people of him?'

'Oh,' said Miss Butterworth, smiling her twisted smile. 'I see what you mean. No, there are no pictures.'

Lenny nodded sadly. Then a monstrous thought sprang into his brain. The shock of it made him shiver. It made him feel hot, then icy cold.

'Clum isn't . . . he isn't . . .' stammered Lenny, 'he isn't alive now, is he? He doesn't still live here, in the Toffee Works? I mean, how long do Toffee Creatures live?'

A scratching sound somewhere above him made his heart leap, his eyes fly upwards. But it was only a pigeon, scrabbling about on the glass dome.

'No,' said Miss Butterworth, choosing her words very carefully. 'He isn't *alive* here now. He perished over a hundred years ago, in the year 1887 to be precise –'

Lenny's breath came out in a long sigh. 'Phew! Thank goodness!'

'– on the night of young Master Harold's tragic accident.'

Miss Butterworth paused, sighed and adjusted her hair-net. It was tiring work bringing Lenny up to date on the Butterworths' family history. Her voice was fading to a whisper. She hadn't used it so much for a long, long time. This boy was from the strange and alien world outside the Toffee Works. But he had toffee in his blood, she was certain. And he'd been specially sent as Butterworth's guardian angel. That gave him the right to know. She decided to finish the job before her voice gave out altogether.

'That night,' she said, 'Harold's mother came to the Toffee Works from Butterworth Towers, a thing she never, ever did. But she had to give Josiah Butterworth an important message. She was all dressed up to go to the ball. She was at her most beautiful. She looked like a fairy princess! She sparkled with jewellery. She had a beautiful silver ballgown on that glittered in the light! Harold and Clum were bewitched by her! Of course, Harold knew he mustn't touch or hug his mother when she was dressed up in all her finery. But poor Clum didn't know that. He wanted to please her. He tried to fetch the fan that she'd left by the door and all the beautiful peacock feathers stuck to his hand. And then when he rushed to take it to her, his other hand touched her silver dress!'

'Oh no! Oh no!' gasped Lenny. 'I bet she went ballistic!'

'She screamed,' agreed Miss Butterworth. 'She had hysterics! She scared poor Clum out of the few wits he had. He hated people shouting and screaming. It really upset him. He was bewildered. He didn't know what he'd done wrong. She shrieked and shrieked at him: "You've ruined my gown, you clumsy, useless creature! Do you know how much that cost?" She took a make-up mirror out of her matching silver evening purse. She held it up. She said, "Look at yourself, you ugly creature! You are a beast, a monster! You should be in a cage, not allowed to mix with decent, civilized people! You are a freak of nature!" And Clum looked in the mirror and saw his own face.'

'And what did he do,' said Lenny in a hushed voice, 'when he found out he wasn't a Butterworth? That he wasn't even human? That he was all warty and looked like something out of a horror film?'

'They say he gave a great, heart-rending croak of anguish. He dashed the mirror to the ground. Then he hopped off to hide in the copper vat. Everyone was rushing around. Fanning Mrs Butterworth, giving her smelling salts. There was a real to-do! Only Harold went after the poor creature, to try and comfort him.'

Lenny looked round the gloomy tower room. He could imagine it happening. Clum rushing here to hide after he'd found out he was a freak. Little Harold hurrying after him –

'That day,' said Miss Butterworth in a voice grim as graveyards, 'the humbug machine was running full pelt – there was a big humbug order to fill. Harold came dashing in. He didn't think. He was only concerned for his friend. Before Clum could reach his vat, Harold threw himself at him to give him a big hug. It was the only time in his short life that the creature had ever been hugged. He was so overjoyed he put his arms round Harold. He lifted him high in the air –'

Lenny's hand flew up to his mouth. 'Oh no, I can't believe it! They stuck together, didn't they?'

'They did. And Harold panicked. He shouted, 'Set me down!' But Clum didn't understand and only squeezed him tighter. Clum didn't know his own strength and poor Harold couldn't breathe. He struggled to get free from the creature's sticky embrace. But he fell –'

Lenny gnawed at his knuckles. It was too awful to think about. 'Harold didn't fall into the humbug machine, did he? Is that what you meant when you said he came to a sticky end?' He looked fearfully at the great machine towering above them. He imagined those great iron paddles whacking the toffee mixture, spitting it out as humbugs, flicking it into tins. The thought of Harold being turned into humbugs was more than he could bear.

'Good heavens,' said Miss Butterworth. 'What gruesome minds you modern children have got! No, Harold didn't fall *into* the machine. He struck his head on one of the paddles as he fell. Clum saw Harold wasn't moving. He cried toffee tears. His poor heart was broken in two.'

'Where was Harold's dad all this time then? Where was Josiah?'

'He rushed in at that very moment with all his toffee workers behind him. They saw what had happened to poor Harold. They saw Clum crouching over him, croaking. And they began howling for revenge!'

'They didn't hurt Clum, did they?'

Miss Butterworth's voice was getting weaker, as she neared the tragic end of her tale.

'Clum slipped past them, out of the tower room, out of the Toffee Works and on to the streets. It was dark and no one could see him. It was winter; there was snow on the ground. More toffee workers joined the chase. They turned into a baying mob with torches and dogs. Clum was terrified and mad with grief. Once they nearly caught him. He turned on them. The poor hunted brute couldn't take any more. He stretched himself up to his full height. He was over seven feet tall! "Careful, he's dangerous!" someone called. So they loosed the dogs but he batted them away with his webbed hands and they ran off yelping into the dark. He got away. He half-hopped, half-ran until he came to the river. There was thick ice covering it, all the way across. He went out on to the ice. The mob wasn't far behind. He could see the blazing torches and hear the men chanting, "Kill the creature! Kill it!" For the first time in his life he was graceful, sliding on the ice, swooping across it like a bird. But in the middle he stopped. The mob crowded on to the river bank, waiting to see what he would do.'

Lenny's face was screwed up in horror. He almost covered up his ears. He didn't want to hear the next bit of the story. But Miss Butterworth went on, relentlessly. Her weary voice was no louder than the rustle of dry leaves. Lenny had to concentrate really hard to hear it.

'They say,' said Miss Butterworth, 'that he turned to look back at the screaming mob, just once. Then he looked up at the shining moon. He seemed to reach out for it, trying to fetch it. He loved silvery things, remember. Then he gave a last despairing croak and jumped up and down on the ice until it cracked beneath him. He let himself slip into the icy water.'

'He could have saved himself!' cried Lenny in anguish. 'He had webbed feet, didn't he? He could have swum!'

'Well, he didn't,' whispered Miss Butterworth, shaking her head. 'He was carried away beneath the ice. The water that day was well below freezing. The mob raced along the bank after him. Further downstream Clum got tangled in some weed. They could see him under the ice. They smashed a hole in it to get to him. When they dragged him out it was far too late. The cold had killed him. He was frozen stiff as stone.'

'Poor Clum,' said Lenny, sniffing hard and wiping a tear away with the bottom of his baggy T-shirt. 'Poor, poor creature. That's a really sad story. I've never heard a story as sad as that one! So what happened to Harold? I expect he was dead as well, wasn't he?'

'No, he wasn't!' protested Miss Butterworth. 'He wasn't dead at all! He was only knocked out.'

'But you said he came to a sticky end! You said so!'

'He did – eventually. But anyhow, the accident made his mother and father notice him –'

'Good!' cried Lenny. 'When they noticed him, did they try and make up for neglecting him? I bet they did, didn't they?'

'No, they didn't,' said Miss Butterworth. 'They packed him off to boarding school.'

'Not in those awful clothes!' groaned Lenny. 'That's criminal, that is!'

'No, no, they did buy him his first set of boy's clothes first – and a cricket bat.'

'But they sent him away!' cried Lenny, who'd never slept away from home for even one night. 'Don't you think that's criminal? That's terrible!'

'Don't worry, it turned out to be the best thing that ever happened to Harold. He was very happy – after he'd got over being sad about Clum, that is. He never came back to the Toffee Works, even in school holidays. He stayed with an auntie in Brighton. And when he was eighteen he left England for good. He went to America to seek his fortune. Many young men did that then. He led a very colourful life, according to the letters he wrote back to his auntie. He had loads of thrilling adventures. He was an Indian chief in the Rocky Mountains, a sheriff in a Wild West town. Then he struck gold in the Yukon and became a rich man and bought a ranch in Texas. He even ran for President!'

'Wow!' said Lenny impressed. He could hardly believe that the mournful child on the toffee tin had gone on to lead such an exciting and wonderful life.

'He lived to be 101 years old! He never came back to the toffee business but, strangely, it was toffee that got him in the end. They say he died trying a dare-devil leap over three cars on his motorbike. Did

I say he was a famous film stuntman too? Just as he was in mid-air, a piece of flying toffee – probably dropped by a passing crow – struck him in the right eye. He lost control and came down like a ton of bricks.'

'What a way to go,' breathed Lenny, shaking his head in admiration.

'Well, you might think so! Personally, I think it was a shame that Harold turned his back on the old family firm. But after what happened to Clum on that dreadful night, he didn't want anything to do with it.'

'I'm not surprised,' muttered Lenny.

'What?' demanded Miss Butterworth.

'Oh, nothing,' said Lenny.

'So,' concluded Miss Butterworth, fixing him with her razor-sharp, lime-drop eyes. 'That's it. That's the secret history of the Butterworths. What do you think about it?'

Lenny couldn't say yet. His feelings were in a whirl. He was sad, deeply sad about Clum, that poor tormented creature who only wanted some kindness. But he was amazed and glad that little Harold had been happy ever after. And didn't have to wear those girly clothes for the rest of his life.

He had loads of questions bubbling away in his brain. But the first one that popped out was: 'Did Josiah ever make another Toffee Creature like Clum?'

'No,' said Miss Butterworth. 'He got a new craze after that. He wasn't interested in Toffee Creatures any more. He went mad on hot air ballooning. It was all the rage, at the time.'

'He didn't make hot air balloons out of treacle toffee did he?'

'No, no,' said Miss Butterworth testily. 'Of course not – do be realistic! But he discovered that our prize-winning treacle toffee was the ideal stuff for patching up holes in balloon fabric –'

'How could he forget Clum that easily?' interrupted Lenny, angrily. 'How could that bloke Josiah be so cruel? He didn't even care about his own creation!'

Miss Butterworth sucked on her teeth thoughtfully. She had one more piece of secret information. 'Shall I tell him?' she asked herself. And she decided, 'Why not?' It would round her story off nicely. And it couldn't do any harm. Not now Clum was dead as a dodo. Besides, she didn't want Lenny to think that the Butterworths were a totally heartless bunch.

'I think Josiah did care about his creation,' she said, 'because he couldn't bear to see Clum thrown back in the river, like a piece of rubbish. He brought him back here, to the Toffee Works –'

Lenny gaped at her like an idiot. He'd never expected this. His overloaded brain just couldn't cope with it. His flesh was creeping all over again! 'Wait a minute!' he roared in protest. 'I just asked you if he was here. And you said NO. You definitely said NO!'

'I *said*,' Miss Butterworth answered him sternly, 'that he wasn't *alive* here. Well, that's quite right. He isn't. But he is *dead* here. His body is down in the basement. It's in my deep freeze. Would you care to take a look?'

Chapter Four

Lenny stood in the Toffee Works kitchen waiting for Miss Butterworth to bring Clum up from the cellar. He stared at the open door where she had disappeared.

'Clump, clump, clump.' He could hear her coming back up the cellar steps in her rubber boots. She seemed to be dragging something with her. He could hear it thumping off every step.

Her voice came up before she did. ''Course,' she was telling him, 'they didn't have deep freezes then. They had ice houses, where they kept the butter cool. Josiah put Clum in there and years passed by and people forgot all about him. I found him when we bought a freezer and pulled the old ice house down –'

Miss Butterworth had to pause for breath. He could hear her wheezing. She was nearly at the top of the steps now. What she was dragging behind her must be very heavy.

Lenny stared and stared at the open cellar door, as if he was hypnotized by it. His eyes were wide with shock, like a rabbit caught in car headlights. Nothing was going on in his mind. Absolutely nothing. It felt numb.

But every nerve in his body was on red alert, quivering. Waiting, just waiting, for what would come through that door.

Miss Butterworth's bottom came through the door first. She backed into the kitchen, hauling her heavy burden with her.

It was a brown sack, thick with ice-crystals. She brushed off a few. The sack was labelled CLUM, in large black letters.

Immediately Lenny's brain sprang into life.

'Hey, wait a minute,' he protested. 'Are you kidding me? I thought Clum was seven feet tall! I thought he was a massive hulking monster!'

'Well, he was,' said Miss Butterworth in her brisk, matter-of-fact voice. 'But, obviously, they couldn't drag his body back through the streets, could they? It might have attracted some attention! And he was frozen stiff, remember. Like a gigantic block of ice.'

'So what did they do to him?' asked Lenny, staring at the sack marked CLUM with horrified fascination. 'How'd they get a seven-foot Toffee Creature into that little sack?'

'Oh, this isn't the only sack with him in it,' said Miss Butterworth. 'There are lots of sacks marked CLUM down there. They couldn't get him into just one sack, could they? No, Josiah had a toffee hammer with him. It was his own personal silver toffee hammer. He carried it around with him everywhere. So they just tapped Clum into convenient chunks, like you would a tray of brazil nut toffee. And they found some sacks and shovelled him in. Then the toffee workers came back here, each of them with a sack slung over his shoulder. And Josiah labelled the sacks and stored them in the ice house. And there they stayed, until I found them.'

She chipped some ice away with her toffee-cutting knife. She forced the neck of the sack open, thrust her hand into it and brought out two small, frozen chunks. She sat them on the table. Lenny peered at them. He expected to feel something. Sadness, revulsion, he didn't quite know what. But he didn't feel anything much when he looked at them. They were just two small lumps of frozen toffee. He couldn't connect them with Clum at all.

Part of him was disappointed. He would have liked to have seen the huge warty, frog-like Toffee Creature. It's not every day you get a chance to see one of those. His friends would be really jealous when he told them. Serve them right for going on holiday!

But part of him was relieved. Clum wasn't real to him yet, not like Harold. But seeing Clum's frozen body, being able to touch it, would have made him very real indeed. Lenny knew it would have given him some terrible nightmares.

'It's better that he's all in bits,' Lenny's common sense told him.

But that flicker of disappointment

wouldn't go away. When Miss Butterworth put those two harmless chunks on the kitchen table, it was a real anti-climax somehow . . .

'Just think,' he said, regretfully. 'What if he were alive now? If Butterworth's toffee had a real, live Toffee Monster! Kids would love that! It'd be brilliant fun!'

'Humm,' said Miss Butterworth. 'Fun isn't the word I'd use. Look, I don't think you quite understand – Clum was a gentle creature at first. A gentle, timid creature. But he changed. He was shouted at, mocked, badly treated. In the end, he didn't trust anyone. Except Harold. When he thought Harold was dead, Clum went out of his mind with rage and grief. He became extremely dangerous. Remember how he turned on the toffee workers? Let me tell you, if he were here now, in this room, we'd be scared out of our wits. You and I would be running to save our skins! So, all in all, it's a good job he's frozen chunks!'

But Lenny didn't want to listen. He had his toffee consultant's hat on. He'd just made up a brilliant advert in his head. 'Kids like being scared,' he assured Miss Butter-worth. 'Clum could go on the telly and give them a real fright. They'd love it! He could look fierce and croak, "BUY BUTTER-WORTH'S TOFFEE – OR ELSE!" And, and, and –'

The words were tumbling out of Lenny's mouth! Minutes ago he'd been speechless with fear. Now he couldn't seem to shut up! 'And Clum could eliminate the opposition –'

'Clum is dead,' interrupted Miss Butter-worth firmly. 'He threw himself into a freez-ing river in 1887.'

But Lenny went babbling on, because, all the time he was talking, he didn't have to sort out all of those mixed-up feelings in his head.

He grabbed his Sparkle Bar off the table. 'You said he could fetch stuff, didn't you? We could show him a Sparkle Bar. We could say, "See that! Go on, have a good sniff at it!" Then we'd say, "Fetch, Clum!" and he'd go out and snatch any Sparkle Bars he saw and bring them back here. So kids would have to buy Butterworth's toffee then, wouldn't they? 'Cos there'd be no Sparkle Bars left anywhere and Butterworth's Toffee would rule the world and –'

BOING, BOING, BOING!

'Whassat!' said Lenny, leaping round like a startled hare. It was as if a spell had been broken.

It was the big Toffee Works clock, on the wall of the kitchen, bonging out the hour.

Lenny stared at the time. 'Oh no!' Instantly, he was back in the real world. He checked his own watch. Said 'Oh no!' again. He looked at his hand, realized he'd been waving the Sparkle Bar round like a prat and dropped it as if it was red hot.

'Where's my bike?' How could he have forgotten about his bike for so long? But there it was, safe, propped up against the wall.

'I got to go,' Lenny blurted out. 'Just look at the time! My mum will be going crazy! I'm going to be in big trouble!' He rushed for his bike. Then he remembered something and turned back. 'I know what I said before about being a toffee consultant and learning toffee throwing and stuff. Well,

I'll come back later. I will. All right?'

But Lenny had no intention of ever coming back.

He wanted to breathe fresh air. He wanted to be outside.

Frantically, he grabbed his bike, wheeled it out of the kitchen, back down the dark corridors and through the gloomy Toffee Museum. He deliberately kept his eyes straight in front. He didn't look to right or left. He didn't want to see young Master Harold's eyes, staring accusingly at him from the toffee tin.

Out on the street he blinked in the strong sunlight. He wheeled his bike to the end of the alley. There were cars out there! And men and women going to work in the factories. Everything looked perfectly normal. He could hardly believe it. Not after the dark and sinister things he'd just learned inside the Toffee Works.

He tried to block them out of his mind. He jumped on his bike and pedalled away like a maniac. He didn't stop once until he was safely back home.

*

71

Back in the Toffee Works kitchen Miss Butterworth sniffed, 'Some guardian angel!' She had already guessed he wasn't planning on coming back. She tied up the neck of the sack and dragged Clum's frozen chunks back down to the freezer.

She told herself she'd been a foolish old woman to have expected anything different. She told herself that she shouldn't have blurted out so much of the Butterworth's secret history to a complete stranger.

But, all the same, there'd been something about that boy.

'He might try to escape from toffee,' she thought. 'But he won't be able to. Toffee is that boy's destiny. He's got toffee in his blood.'

She was parched after all that talking and very tired. She came up from the cellar and wearily climbed the stairs to her tiny parlour to have a sit-down and a cup of tea.

Her tiredness had made her forgetful. She'd forgotten the two lumps of Clum left on the kitchen table. And she had taken the toffee pans off the stove but she'd forgotten to turn off the rings.

Gradually the kitchen got hotter. It was stifling. The frozen chunks of brazil nut toffee began to thaw out. Soon they were lying in little pools of water.

Upstairs, Miss Butterworth was having a nap in her only comfy chair.

Downstairs the toffee chunks were getting softer. At last, they were completely defrosted.

Then one of them started to twitch.

Chapter Five

When Lenny got home the house smelled of milky baby and smelly nappies. Mum was kneeling down in the living-room changing his baby sister. The baby's tiny, twiggy arms and legs were waving wildly about in the air, like a cockroach stuck on its back.

'How can anything so little make such a big pong,' said Lenny, wrinkling his nose. 'It's disgusting!'

'Pass me that baby cream,' said Mum, looking up.

'Huh,' thought Lenny. 'She hasn't even noticed I'm late. I needn't have nearly killed myself racing back home!'

'When are you going to make toffee apples again?' he demanded.

'What?' His mum looked up, surprised by his question, and by the angry tone of his voice.

'Toffee apples? I didn't think you even liked them. I haven't got time to make toffee apples. I'm run off my feet with the baby.'

'Have I got toffee in my blood then?' demanded Lenny, in the same angry, accusing voice. 'Have you got *time* to tell me that?'

His mum squatted back on her heels, sensing trouble. She had thick white baby cream all over her hands. 'What are you talking about, Lenny?' she sighed. 'You're not making any sense.'

Lenny was about to go 'Huh!' again and stamp his way upstairs when, out of the blue, his mum said, 'Actually, your Granny Wang told me something about toffee once.' She frowned and shook her head. 'It was about *somebody* in our family –'

As she wiped the baby cream off her hands, her face seemed lost in thought. Her eyes were far away, searching in the past. Lenny was pleased to see that, even though the baby was whimpering like a kitten, Mum wasn't taking any notice of it.

At last Mum smiled. 'I know!' she said. 'I remember now. Your Granny Wang said that *her* grandma, who lived all her life in China, was famous for being a brilliant toffee maker.'

'Honest?' said Lenny thrilled. He waited for Mum to say more. He darted his baby sister a warning glance, as if to say, 'Don't you dare interrupt! Me and Mum are talking about something important!'

Mum's face lit up with memories. 'Granny Wang's granny,' she said, 'was a tiny little lady. Granny Wang's got a really, really old photo of her somewhere, in a jacket embroidered with dragons. Granny Wang told me that, when she was a little girl, she would go and watch *her* gran spinning toffee. She says it was an amazing sight.'

'Spinning toffee,' said Lenny, speaking quickly in case his baby sister butted in. 'How'd you do that?'

'Well, I don't know exactly,' said Mum, rocking to and fro on her heels, remembering. 'But Granny Wang says it looked like magic. She says she loved to watch it. Her granny could take a lump of toffee and spin it out into long thin strands like candy floss and then she'd make it into things.'

'Things? What kind of things?' said Lenny with half an eye on the baby, who was just opening her mouth to squawk. 'Please keep quiet,' he begged the baby, inside his head.

'Oh,' said Mum, 'things – like toffee sculptures. She made waterlily flowers. You know, for special occasions and banquets. And she made swans. Life-size swans, out of spun toffee. Can you imagine it? They must have been beautiful. They must have looked like they were made out of glass.'

'I'd like to have seen them!' said Lenny excitedly.

'So would I,' said Mum, smiling warmly at him. 'I really would like to have seen one –'

'Waaaaa!' went the baby, distracting Mum's attention.

But Lenny didn't care about the crying now. He had the information he needed.

His mind was racing, he was thrilled at this new knowledge. He carried it around in his mind like a sparkling jewel.

'Life-size swans out of toffee! For special occasions and banquets!' he reminded himself, as he went into the kitchen to zap some chips in the microwave.

When he'd ridden away from the Toffee Works he'd been sure that he was never going back. But what he'd learned about Granny Wang's granny had changed all that.

Miss Butterworth wouldn't have been at all surprised. She was still asleep in her comfy chair back at the Toffee Works. But if you'd woken her up and told her, she would have looked at you with her sharp little lime-drop eyes and snapped, 'I could've told *you* that! It's obvious that toffee runs in that boy's family!'

Down in the Toffee Works kitchen very strange things were going on.

The two thawed-out chunks were squirming all over the table top. They looked like fat, sticky brown slugs. But they had no eyes or ears or mouths. They had no brains either – just clumps of nerve cells. They couldn't think, they just reacted to chemical signals. They were very simple life forms, like the squidgy things that lived in primeval swamps. But there was one vital difference. They were bits of Clum. They couldn't think and feel like Clum. But imprinted inside them, deep in their primitive genes, were some of Clum's behaviour patterns.

Instinctively, they reared up and seemed to test the air. They seemed to get very excited. They recognized that potent chemical mix! Instantly, they reacted. They locked on to the Sparkle Bar like miniature homing missiles. Moving horribly fast, like speeded-up loopy caterpillars, they shot across the table. They wriggled down the table leg, leaving a sticky toffee trail behind them.

Whop! They lunged at the Sparkle Bar. It was on the floor where Lenny had dropped it. They glued themselves to it like sucker fish. 'Fetch!' Lenny had cried, waving his Sparkle Bar about, not for a second guessing that the Clum chunks were programmed to do just that.

The toffee slugs hauled their prize back to the table top. Then, suddenly, they dropped it. They reared up again and began waving from side to side like tiny cobras. Their amazingly sensitive radar had detected, very faintly, a chemical signal, coming through an open window high in the kitchen wall. Another Sparkle Bar! Immediately, they set off to fetch it.

The Sparkle-seeking pair flowed across the floor, up the wall and through the window. Soon, they were outside. Slithering along in the gutter through the industrial estate. Nothing could stop them. Nothing could get in their way. They were on a mission.

Chapter Six

Almost straight away, they ran into problems.

One of the toffee slugs fell down a drain. But it didn't matter. It was still locked on to its target. It could still detect that Sparkle Bar chemistry, even in the disgusting pong of the sewers. Unstoppable, it swam on through the sewage system. Ratty eyes glowed from the darkness, as it swirled past on the sludgy water.

The other toffee slug met with an even worse accident. Splat, it was run over by a Volvo. Pressed deep in the tyre treads, it lost the Sparkle scent. It was carried off, spinning round and round on the tyre, to the car park of the local cinema.

*

At number two, Wordsworth Road, Gemma had locked herself in the bathroom. It was the only place you could be private. The only place to escape from her quarrelsome little brothers, who pestered the life out of her. She was perched on the fluffy pink toilet seat cover, reading her magazine. She gave a deep sigh of contentment. Peace and quiet at last! With any luck she could stay here for ages, until her mum hammered on the door and yelled, 'Gemma! What on earth are you doing in there?'

She turned a page in her magazine and began reading her horoscope. 'Today,' it said, 'you should expect the unexpected!' Still reading, she took a Sparkle Bar out of her pocket.

She thought of all the unexpected things she could expect.

But that didn't include a toffee slug, clinging under the toilet rim, waiting to snaffle her Sparkle Bar.

The toffee slug's swim through the sewers hadn't tired it out. It never got tired. It never gave up. It was as unstoppable as

Terminator. Only it didn't hunt people. It hunted Sparkle Bars.

Gemma ripped a tiny corner of silver wrapping off the Sparkle Bar. Down the toilet, the toffee slug quivered.

Before Gemma knew what was happening, it squeezed itself under the toilet seat. It looped, quick as a weasel, up her back, down her arm and snatched the Sparkle Bar out of her hand. She didn't even scream. She just sat there, with her mouth wide open, staring at her empty fist.

'Mum! Mum! Mum!' she yelled. Feet came pounding up the stairs. 'What's the matter?' But the Sparkle-swiper was long gone. There was nothing to show it had been there at all, just a glistening trail, like a snail trail, on the outside of Gemma's red jumper.

The slug swam back through the sewers. The Sparkle Bar was safely secured on its sticky back. And, as it swam, the neon wrapper glimmered in the blackness, like a silver beacon.

The cinema was jumping with children. It was a matinée performance. Daniel was sitting in the back row with his girlfriend. He was nervous. It was his very first date. He'd spent ages beforehand, spraying on deodorant, putting hair gel on his hair. He didn't want anything to go wrong.

He had bought her some popcorn. He had even bought her a Sparkle Bar. It was in his pocket. He was saving it for later.

Out in the car park, the second toffee slug was a bit the worse for wear. It was still plugged deep into the car tyre. But it was not defeated. Nothing could stop it in its quest for Sparkle Bars. And the Sparkle Bar chemistry was very strong indeed. In the cinema, Sparkle Bars fizzed in dozens of mouths, turning dozens of sets of teeth bright blue. Under seats the wrappers rustled, like silver autumn leaves.

The toffee slug began dragging itself out of the tyre treads. It left glops of itself behind. But that didn't matter. It still knew what it had to do.

It crept across the car park, past the eagle eyes of the usherette and into the darkened cinema. The Sparkle scent was overpowering! It was coming from all directions! For a moment the toffee slug dithered. Its radar system was overloaded. It didn't know where to go first.

Then, in the nearest seat, Daniel took his Sparkle Bar out of his pocket to give to his girlfriend. The toffee slug waved from side to side like a charmed snake. Then it shot up the back of Daniel's seat.

Daniel did feel something gloopy on his head. He felt it slide down the back of his neck. But it didn't alarm him. He just thought he'd put on too much hair gel. His mother was always telling him off about that. 'Daniel, your head looks like an oil slick.'

He was busy trying to get things right. He didn't think he'd made any bad mistakes so far. She might even go out with him again. He wondered if he was supposed to give her a kiss. Would she get mad if he didn't? Or would she get mad if he did? He didn't know what to do. His mind was tying itself into knots. He didn't notice that, as he handed the Sparkle Bar over, something sticky and strange dive-bombed on to it, like a tiny toffee torpedo.

'Have a Sparkle Bar,' Daniel said. He was pleased with how cool his voice sounded.

'*Aaaargh!*' A shriek of horror came out of the darkness. It nearly burst his eardrums. Everyone twisted round in their seats to look.

'How disgusting!' protested his girlfriend, in a voice that rang round the cinema.

Daniel cringed. He tried to fold himself up in his seat so no one could see him.

'What's the matter?' he hissed, in a panic. 'What have I done? What have I done?'

'This Sparkle Bar is revolting! It's all covered with goo! It's all covered with sticky stuff. What have you got in your pocket? You boys are really disgusting creatures!'

Afterwards, when the lights came on again, Daniel searched for the Sparkle Bar on the floor. He would have liked to see what was on it! He couldn't think what he'd had in his pocket. Unless there was some half-chewed gum he'd forgotten about. Or some of that tub of 'Silly Putty' he'd bought in a joke shop last week.

He looked at the seat by his side. It was empty. His girlfriend had rushed away to sit with her friends. Surprisingly, he felt quite relieved.

'I don't think I'm ready for girlfriends yet,' he decided.

The first toffee slug popped up out of a drain. It joined the second one on its way back to the Toffee Works. It was getting dark now. No one spotted them in the gutter as they shuffled through crisp packets and crushed drink cans with their Sparkle Bars on their backs.

One motorist thought, 'What's that?' as he drove along. It looked like the gleam of a wild creature's eyes, reflected in his car headlights. But he soon forgot all about it.

In her tiny parlour above the Toffee Works kitchen, Miss Butterworth was finally waking up from her nap.

'It's dark!' she thought, switching on a light. She was annoyed with herself for sleeping for such a long time. She still had more toffee throwing to do. She eased her aching bones out of the chair and went downstairs to the kitchen.

'You're getting old!' she told herself. 'And stupid too!' she said sternly. She couldn't help remembering that boy, Lenny. How she'd blabbed all the Butterworth secrets to him. How she'd persuaded herself that he, a mere child, could save her precious Toffee Works from ruin.

'Dozy old bat,' she mumbled, shaking her head. 'Such daft flights of fancy. Such daft dreams! It's not like you at all, Araminta. You're getting soft!'

Araminta was Miss Butterworth's first name. It had been chosen in honour of Butterworth's peppermint toffee, which had won the 'Best Toffee' prize the year she was born. But no one had called her Araminta for fifty years or more.

'And you've left the stove on,' she said, hobbling stiffly across the kitchen. 'You're lucky the whole place didn't catch fire. I think you're losing your grip!'

Miss Butterworth was often hard on people. She told them what she thought. She didn't mince her words. But she was hardest of all on herself.

She switched off the stove. 'Phew, it's hot

in here,' she said, taking off her white hat to fan herself. Then she saw the three Sparkle Bars heaped on the kitchen table like a little offering. And the two toffee slugs standing by as if they were guarding them.

'Eh?' she said to herself. She thought she was still asleep, still dreaming. She reached out to touch the hot stove. Ow, that hurt. She was wide awake all right.

She peered at the two sticky pieces of Clum. They were very lively now. Squirming about, stretching themselves into long, skinny strings like worms do, then twanging back into fat little lumps.

'Well, would you look at that?' she murmured to herself.

She looked next at the three Sparkle Bars: 'Where'd they come from?' And her shrewd mind began working away like mad. She was trying to remember what Lenny, her ex-toffee consultant, had said before he rode off on his bike. Something like: 'If he were alive now, we'd show Clum a Sparkle Bar. We'd say "Fetch!" And he'd go out and snatch every one he saw.'

Still puzzled, she tried an experiment.

She threw one of the Sparkle Bars on the floor. 'Fetch!' she said.

She didn't expect anything to happen. And she had already started to scold herself, 'Dozy old . . .' when a toffee slug nipped down the table leg, stuck itself to the Sparkle Bar and brought it back up to the table, neat as you please.

She tried it twice more. 'Fetch! Fetch!' and when it worked every time a slow, rather sneaky grin spread over her face. 'Well, well, well . . .' she said thoughtfully.

She put the stove on again. And then, one by one, she began to haul all the frozen sacks of Clum up from the cellar. It took her a long time. There were twenty-two of them . . .

Miss Butterworth was terribly behind the times. She'd been practically a hermit for years and years. All her groceries, everything she needed, were delivered to the Toffee Works. She hardly ever went out. She didn't have a TV. She didn't know that, at any supermarket, there were shelves full of sweets. Sweets that had glossy wrappers and special offers and adverts with catchy jingles just like Sparkle Bars did. She thought Sparkle Bars were her main rival. Lenny had made it seem like that. And she didn't know any different.

'Well, I'll soon get shot of them,' panted Miss Butterworth, as she dragged yet another sack up the steps. 'When I send this lot out, there won't be a Sparkle Bar left anywhere in this city!'

It didn't take long to defrost the chunks. Miss Butterworth turned all the rings on full blast, until the kitchen was like a furnace. Soon the floor was alive with a wriggling sea of toffee slugs.

Miss Butterworth didn't know about DNA and genetically programmed behaviour. She didn't know she was dealing with what modern science would call *smart* toffee. So she addressed the chunks like this: 'I don't know what you are,' she said. 'I know you're not Clum. You're not even mini-Clums. You don't have his brains and his feelings. You don't look like him. You are only his poor body bits. But nevertheless I believe that somewhere inside each of you, a trace of the mighty Clum remains!'

She picked up the three Sparkle Bars. She waved them in their shining silvery wrappers above her head. As one, the toffee slugs writhed in response to the chemical signal.

'These,' declaimed Miss Butterworth dramatically, 'are the deadly enemies of Butterworth's Toffee! If it wasn't for these, we wouldn't be in the pickle we're in. Fetch! Do you hear me? Fetch! Go out there and bring me every one of these dratted bars. *Every single one.*'

She swept her arm towards the door. She knew she was being really over-the-top. But she just couldn't help it. Toffee always aroused her strongest, wildest passions.

She rushed to the door of the Toffee Works and threw it wide open.

'Go, my beauties, and fetch me Sparkle Bars!' she cried.

As one, the huge toffee army moved to obey. Thousands and thousands of chunks of Clum trooped into the night, and scattered throughout the suburbs.

Chapter Seven

Relentlessly, the smart toffee slugs began tracking down Sparkle Bars. Sometimes they brought them back to the Toffee Works in ones and twos. Snatched from under the pillow of a sleeping child, or from under the nose of a night-duty nurse who was just about to swallow one as a snack.

Sometimes they brought back hundreds. They squeezed themselves like brown toothpaste under the locked doors of supermarkets. They pounced on the Sparkle Bars like packs of hungry wolves! They cleared the shelves! They came looping back through the midnight streets with the Sparkle Bars on their backs, like an army of glow-worms, glittering in the dark.

In the Toffee Works kitchen Miss Butter-worth greeted them as they slithered in, dropped the bars and then slithered back out again, in search of more. The gleaming silver heap on the table rose higher and higher. 'Fetch! Fetch!' cried Miss Butterworth, with a devilish gleam in her eyes. She didn't know how this was happening, why it was happening. But she didn't care. All that mattered was that, with Sparkle Bars gone, Butterworth's toffee was going to be the nation's number one sweet again.

Lenny was having a bad night. His brain was like a kaleidoscope. Pictures were tumbling around in there. Some of them were delightful. Some of them were nightmarish. He saw Miss Butterworth toffee-throwing, making sparkling golden rainbows in the kitchen. He saw Granny Wang's granny spinning toffee swans, as fragile as crystal. Then he saw Clum, his poor froggy face full of pain, turning for one last look at the mob before slipping into the icy water.

'It's no good,' thought Lenny. 'I can't sleep!'

He wrapped himself in his duvet and shuffled to his bedroom window. He dragged his curtains aside. He'd been lying awake so long he expected to see a pinky dawn. But no, it was still the dead of night. The sky was navy blue and sprinkled with stars.

He was about to go back to bed again when something out in the street caught his eye.

The pavement was alive! It was rippling, like the sea! He blinked. He thought it was just a trick of the light. But no, he could still see silver waves.

'Hang on,' he thought, 'Those aren't waves, those are . . .'

Immediately horrible suspicions clawed at his mind. He tried to ignore them. He pulled his T-shirt and jeans on. He slipped his feet into his shoes.

He knew he shouldn't be doing this. He knew he would be in big, big trouble if anyone caught him going out at this time of night.

'Shhhhh!' he thought as he tiptoed downstairs. 'Don't let them hear you!'

But there was no danger of that. Mum and Dad had only just got the baby to sleep. Now they were making up for lost sleep themselves. A brass band tooting in their ears probably wouldn't have woken them up.

Lenny grabbed his bike from the hallway and let himself out the front door. He wheeled the bike into the street.

He couldn't believe what he saw. He was standing in the middle of a mass migration of Sparkle Bars. They didn't stop for him. They flowed round him as if he were a rock, closed ranks and carried on their way. They were moving in the direction of the Toffee Works.

'Whaa –' gasped Lenny, gazing after the silver stream. 'What's going on?'

Then he said, 'Ugh. What have I trodden in?'

There was a nutty mess on the bottom of his trainer. But even as he watched, it prised itself out of the grips on the sole of his shoe. It reformed itself into a slug-shape and fell to the ground, where it wriggled purposefully away.

Shocked and curious, Lenny tried to pick up a mobile Sparkle Bar. At first he couldn't rip it away from the pavement. Then, plop, he de-suckered it. He turned it over. Instantly, his face paled to a ghastly white.

'Chunks of Clum!' he said. 'And they're taking these Sparkle Bars somewhere. What's going on?'

He leapt on to his bike. Avoiding the snaky trail of Sparkle Bars, he pedalled off down the pavement heading for the Toffee Works.

'What's Miss Butterworth playing at?' he thought, grimly.

He knew, just knew, that she was behind all this.

When he burst into the Toffee Works kitchen, Miss Butterworth was standing in the middle of it, gazing at a mountain of Sparkle Bars that reached almost to the ceiling and spilled over, like a silver waterfall, on to the floor.

Like busy ants, the smart toffee came trooping across the kitchen adding Sparkle Bars to the pile.

Miss Butterworth turned to Lenny. She

didn't seem surprised to see him. 'Look at that!' she said, proudly. 'You wouldn't believe it, would you? Those defrosted bits of Clum did that! Amazing, isn't it? I waved a Sparkle Bar at them. I said, 'Fetch!' and off they went, good as gold –'

'Wait a minute, wait a minute,' begged Lenny, with a wild look in his eyes. 'I think my brain's going to explode! I think the world's going crazy! You've got to tell me what's going on! How did these bits of Clum come alive in the first place?'

'Well,' said Miss Butterworth. 'It was quite simple really. They got frisky as soon as they thawed out, don't ask me why –'

'I know why!' interrupted Lenny. A great light had suddenly come on in his brain. It dazzled him with its brilliance. 'Did you see that programme on telly last week – about deep freezing living things? Haven't you heard of cryogenics?'

'Eh?' said Miss Butterworth, looking blank.

'Well, you've heard of frogs, haven't you?'

'Of course I have,' said Miss Butterworth testily. 'Didn't I tell you? My grandad

Josiah was something of an expert on frogs.'

'That's just the point!' said Lenny. 'That's just what I'm trying to tell you! I think one of his frogs hopped into the toffee mixture. It might even have been put in deliberately!'

'That could never happen at our Toffee Works,' said Miss Butterworth appalled. 'These kitchens are spotless! No frogs allowed!'

'I'm talking about up in the tower room, where Josiah did his experiments,' said Lenny, impatiently. 'I'm talking about in 1887, when Clum was made.'

He could see it all in his mind – the tower room, on the night of the great storm. A big bubbling brew of sugar, brazil nuts, froggy DNA and any other secret ingredients the genius Josiah had slung into the vat. All churning around, blasted by massive mega-volts of electricity. Molecules zipping about in a frantic chemical dance, making a zillion combinations!

It was hardly surprising that it cooked up something like Clum.

'Frogs can deep freeze themselves,' said

Lenny, in growing excitement. 'I saw about it on the telly! They can go as stiff as ice lollies and still come to life. It's a really neat trick! It's all got to do with blood sugar, they need loads of sugar in their bodies to do it. Just think how much sugar a Toffee Creature's got. He should be able to deep freeze really well!'

'Are you telling me,' said Miss Butterworth, 'that Clum was never really dead? Are you telling me he's still alive?'

Lenny frowned. He wasn't too sure about this. They hadn't covered things like this in the telly programme he saw.

'Well,' he said finally, 'I suppose if he hadn't been tapped into chunks with a toffee hammer then he would be alive, wouldn't he? But he was, so only these *bits* of him are alive.'

'Thank goodness,' said Miss Butterworth, with a heartfelt sigh of relief. She could cope with bits of Clum. They were just brainless little slugs. But a whole Clum? A thinking, feeling Toffee Creature who, before he froze solid, hated all humans except young Master Harold? She could see some problems there. She could see dreadful danger . . .

But Lenny wasn't thinking about danger. He was thrilled with his own brainwork, springboarding from one great idea to another.

''Course,' he went on, smiling as he said it because this idea was his craziest yet, 'it's a good job, if Josiah put the frog in deliberately, that he didn't know about sponges. You know, the kind that live under the sea. There are these sponges, I mean, they're brilliant. I saw about them on this programme as well. You can cut them up into weeny bits. You can even grind them up into powder but they'll still join up together to make one big sponge. It's a good job Josiah didn't know about them, isn't it? Ha, ha, ha, it's a good job he didn't chuck one of them in, isn't –'

Abruptly, Lenny stopped chuckling. Miss Butterworth was staring at him, her face sickly grey with shock.

'Oh no!' cried Lenny, appalled. 'Don't tell me! Don't tell me that –'

'Yes,' Miss Butterworth whispered,

nodding. 'You've guessed it. He was an expert on sponges as well.'

'Why did he have to be such a clever-clogs!' wailed Lenny in despair.

As one, they turned to look at the kitchen floor. While they'd been talking the silvery flood had slowed to a trickle. Now only one lonely bit of Clum came looping towards them, bringing its Sparkle Bar to add to the pile. It unstuck itself from the bar, turned and hurried out of the kitchen.

They waited and waited. No more smart toffee came in.

'Where are they all?' demanded Miss Butterworth, angrily. 'They can't have finished yet. This can't be every Sparkle Bar in the city! Not by a long chalk!'

Lenny felt his mouth go suddenly dry. He swallowed nervously, once, twice.

'I think,' he said, 'that I know where to find them.'

Miss Butterworth followed him out of the kitchen, to the twisty steps that led to the tower room. The steps were slimed with sticky trails. They peered upwards into the gloom.

'I know they're up there,' hissed Lenny. His hands were shaking badly. He had to scrunch them up into fists to stop them.

'Well, I'm going up,' said Miss Butterworth, in her most determined, no-nonsense voice. She straightened her hair-net. She put a rubber boot on the bottom step.

Lenny didn't know if she was brave. Or if she had no imagination. But, either way, he couldn't let her go up those stairs alone.

'I'm coming too,' he told her. And he followed her up into the darkness.

Chapter Eight

Lenny's mind was like a big, black hole. He daren't allow himself to think about what they might find at the top of the stairs. Or he'd turn around, start running and never stop . . .

Miss Butterworth clumped on ahead, her knobbly hand grasping the stair-rail.

'Doesn't anything scare her?' thought Lenny. It was as if she was hardly human.

He couldn't see in the dark that she was gripping the stair-rail so tightly that her knuckles stood out, white as bone.

At the top of the stairs they had to tiptoe, so they didn't squelch any toffee slugs. The slugs were flattening themselves like leeches, posting themselves under the tower room door . . .

'That's where they're all going,' said Lenny in a shaky whisper, jabbing his thumb at the door.

'I can see that!' snapped Miss Butterworth. She sounded really frosty. But Lenny forgave her. Because he suddenly realized that she was just as scared as he was.

'Right! Here goes!' said Miss Butterworth. She took a deep breath. She pushed the door of the tower room open. They stepped over some slithering bits of Clum. They were inside the room.

Murky moonlight came in through the glass dome. It filled the tower room with spooky grey light.

Lenny looked round, his heart thumping.

But it all seemed very quiet and peaceful. The cupboard that held young Master Harold's clothes, his broken toy horse, the huge hulking humbug machine – everything was in its right place. Nothing seemed changed or disturbed. Even the bits of Clum had stopped climbing the stairs now. There were none of them wriggling across the floor.

It was so still that Lenny and Miss Butterworth could hear their own breathing. They looked round again. They looked up through the grimy glass dome. Sailing high in the sky, they could see the silvery disc of the moon –'

They looked at each other, their eyes full of questions.

Lenny was going to open his mouth to speak when, suddenly, a lone toffee slug came scurrying through the door. It had just been to the kitchen to dump its Sparkle Bar. It was in a great rush, as if it was late for a very important appointment. It seemed to know exactly where it was going. Lenny stared at it. He couldn't take his eyes off it, as it shuffled through the dust and disappeared behind the humbug machine.

'Where –?' was the only word he managed to get out of his mouth.

Then a great dark shape rose up from behind the humbug machine. It was massive, a giant, it seemed to fill the room.

It looked like a writhing mountain of maggots. But they weren't maggots. They were the toffee slugs. They were jiggling about in a frenzy, trying to sort themselves out, trying to assemble themselves into something . . .

A hand appeared from the squirming mass. Then two hands, then a lumpy arm. The hands flexed their webbed fingers. They groped around.

Lenny stared and stared. His brain shrieked, 'Run!' But his legs felt like trickling sand. They couldn't run. They couldn't even keep him upright. He sagged against the cupboard, dizzy with shock.

A face seemed to push itself out of the jostling slugs. It was froggy, warty, with great goggly eyes. A face from your very worst nightmare. It turned its great head around. It smacked its sticky toffee lips.

'Kerr-oak!'

'Clum!' Miss Butterworth tried to say, but no sound came out, her lips only mouthed the word.

The creature moved out from behind the humbug machine. Some toffee slugs hadn't found their right places yet. His warty skin crawled as they shifted about.

He scratched at it with his webbed hands. He was hideous, a monster. Only his golden-flecked eyes seemed human. But they weren't working properly yet. They were like a new-born baby's; they couldn't focus. Clum stared blindly around, his skin twitching and jumping. He was croaking softly now, like a frog in a pond on a summer night:

'Kerroak, kerroak.'

Then he began to sniff. He lifted his massive head. His froggy nostrils flared. He had smelled – humans.

And suddenly, his brain cells speeded up. You could practically see him making connections. Humans – they had scorned him, rejected him, hounded him to death. Pictures flashed through his brain – the screaming mob, the dogs, the blazing torches, the black, icy water. It made him croak out in terror all over again.

He lumbered about, sniffing out that hated and feared human smell. At the same time, his eyes snapped into focus. And he saw Lenny and Miss Butterworth, cowering against the cupboard.

'The door,' hissed Lenny. 'The door.'

But Clum saw their eyes sneaking towards

it. He moved on his springy legs, three clumsy hops to the right, to cut off their escape route.

'Get away from us, you great ugly freak!' shrieked Lenny, nearly out of his mind with terror.

Instantly he knew he shouldn't have done that. It was a big, big mistake. He shouldn't have screamed at Clum. He should have been gentle and quiet, as Clum had once been before he was so mistreated.

He shouldn't have called him an ugly freak. It triggered memories deep in Clum's mind. Of a woman in a sparkling silver dress. How she had thrust a mirror at him and shown him – himself. Clum ran a webbed hand over his warty features. His face twisted up in despair. He roared a great rumbling croak that made the glass dome quiver. Then he started to smash up Josiah's laboratory, as if in revenge for his own creation.

He shot out his arm – it seemed to stretch and stretch like a toffee rope! It swept aside all the flasks and glass tubes. They crashed to the floor and shattered. He picked up a wooden bench and flung it against the wall. He attacked the humbug machine next. He glued himself to it like a great sticky octopus and began to rock it. Its paddles swiped madly at empty air. The floorboards sagged with the strain.

'What's he doing?' cried Miss Butterworth.

'I dunno. He's trying to wreck the place! Let's get out of here!'

'No!' said Miss Butterworth, clutching his arm. 'If that floor gives way that machine will crash through my living-room, through my kitchen! Think of the damage! My Toffee Works will be rubble! We've got to stop him!'

'You stop him,' thought Lenny, as he crept crab-like towards the door.

The Toffee Creature was still battling with the iron machine. But one eye swivelled round. He gave an angry croak of protest. A toffee arm snaked out –

'Oh no!' thought Lenny, diving to the floor.

Lucky for him that Clum wasn't very co-ordinated. He missed Lenny completely.

His hand closed round something else that was lying there in the dust. It was young Master Harold's broken toy horse.

Clum's toffee arm reeled it in. He held the toy horse inches from his nose, staring at it. Then suddenly, his craggy face softened. Toffee tears, like liquid amber, dribbled down his chin. He cradled the horse in his sticky arms. He had remembered Harold, the only human who'd been kind to him. And, just as quickly as he'd remembered him, he'd remembered that he, Clum, had killed him.

Miss Butterworth was just thinking, 'Good, he's calmed down,' when suddenly Clum put the horse down. He attacked the humbug machine even more ferociously. With desperate savagery, he wrenched it off the floor.

'What's he playing at now?' gasped Miss Butterworth. 'He'll kill us all!' She was clinging on tight to the cupboard. The whole tower room was rocking! Loud cracks, like gunfire, came from the floorboards. Everywhere, flasks were exploding like glass grenades.

But, in spite of his terror, Lenny understood. He knew what Clum was playing at.
He found he could read Clum's mind. He
could think like a Toffee Creature! It came
really easily to him.

'Those paddle things whacked Harold's
head!' he yelled at Miss Butterworth
through the din. 'He's mad at them, isn't
he? He wants to break the machine to bits!
He wants to break everything to bits!'

Clum gave another great heave:
'Kerroak!' His toffee pecs bulged like Pop-
eye's. The tower room shuddered and
groaned – that floor wouldn't hold much
longer. The cupboard door flew open. A
Scottish cap came flying out, its blue and
red ribbons gaily fluttering.

Miss Butterworth stared at it. Suddenly,
her eyes flickered with hope.

'Put Harold's clothes on!' she yelled at
Lenny.

'What?' Lenny yelled back. 'What did
you say?' He thought his ears were playing
tricks.

'Hurry up!' insisted Miss Butterworth.
'Make him think Harold is still alive!'

'You must be joking!' cried Lenny, appalled. 'No way! I'm off!' He staggered towards the door. But the floor bucked beneath him and he ended up sprawled full length in the dust.

He felt Miss Butterworth's thin, wiry arms hauling him up.

'For heaven's sake!' she thundered, as a floorboard sprang up and nails ricocheted round the room. 'It's too late to escape. Any minute now, my Toffee Works will be a heap of bricks! PUT THESE CLOTHES ON!'

She waved the lacy dress at him like a flag. She slapped Harold's boots down on the bench.

Things could hardly be grimmer. They were trapped in a tower room with a distraught Toffee Creature on a wrecking spree.

But amazingly, Lenny still hesitated. 'Not that cap!' he was thinking. 'Not that lacy frock. No way!' He'd rather die!

Almost.

'At least none of my friends will see me,' he thought. They were all on holiday. That decided him.

'What are you waiting for!' roared Miss Butterworth above the din of croaking and splintering wood. 'Hurry up! Get those clothes on!'

Lenny pulled Harold's dress on over his jeans and T-shirt. He kicked off his trainers, buttoned on Harold's boots. They were too tight. But that was the least of his problems. He yanked his woolly cap off, plonked Harold's tartan cap on his head.

'He's not going to be fooled! I don't look anything like Harold! Harold had golden curly hair!' Lenny's own hair was spiky and black.

'Just wait!' hissed Miss Butterworth. 'Clum's not very bright. He's thick as two short planks! And he needs glasses – his eyesight's not very good. Go on!' She pushed Lenny forward. 'Go on, call out his name.'

Lenny tottered towards the rampaging Toffee Creature. 'Clum!' he said, his voice quavering with fear. 'It's me, Clum, young Master Harold.'

And all the time he was thinking, 'This isn't gonna work! It isn't gonna work!'

Clum turned round. First he looked puzzled. His froggy face was one big question mark.

Then he gave a great, delighted croak of recognition.

He completely forgot the humbug machine. He just let it drop. Crash! It bounced off the floor. He hopped forward, peered very closely at Lenny's face. Lenny felt as if his heart would stop. Clum was so close he could smell his sweet toffee breath, see the slugs still wriggling around, see his goggly, gold-flecked eyes.

Lenny stared, fascinated, at those eyes. They weren't dumb beast's eyes. Clum wasn't as thick as all that. There was some kind of intelligence shining in them, Lenny was sure of it.

At the moment, they were bright with tears. Clum was crying again. But tears of joy this time. He croaked a greeting. He hopped forwards and spread his arms wide as if to give Lenny a big hug. Instinctively, Lenny drew back. Clum looked wounded.

'Sticky!' said Lenny, just as Harold might

have done. 'You're all sticky. I'll get stuck, won't I?'

He wasn't sure how to talk to Clum. How do you talk to a Toffee Creature? He was shouting now, as if Clum was deaf. Using simple words, like you would to a little child.

But Clum seemed to understand. Instead of hugging him, Clum showed his affection the only way he could. He fetched something. It was Harold's little wooden horse.

'Err, thanks,' said Lenny, awkwardly. The horse was all sticky. Everything Clum fetched was always sticky. But Lenny pretended not to notice. He decided that's what Harold would have done.

'Thanks for fetching it for me,' he told Clum. He trundled the lopsided horse about a bit, just to show how pleased he was.

'Kerroak!'

'Beautiful!' whispered Miss Butterworth. 'It's worked beautifully! He's like a lamb. You've got him in the palm of your hand!'

She spoke too soon. Just because he'd found Harold, that didn't mean Clum had forgotten the unkindness of other humans. He remembered it, far, far too well.

His goggly eye whipped round to Miss Butterworth. He gave a quick savage croak and lashed out at her with a finny hand.

'No, leave her alone!' cried Lenny. 'Come on, come with me.'

He didn't know why he said the last bit. It was right off the top of his head. He just wanted to get Clum away. He was far too dangerous. He wanted to get him away from Miss Butterworth so he didn't hurt her. Away from the tower room which held so many dreadful memories for him.

It surprised him that he wasn't more terrified. But he wasn't. He felt in control. He felt certain Clum wouldn't harm him. Not as long as he thought he, Lenny, was young Master Harold.

'Come on,' said Lenny to Clum. 'Let's go walkies.'

Like an obedient dog, Clum followed. He hopped eagerly after Lenny.

'Where are you taking him?' said Miss Butterworth, very very softly, so she didn't distract Clum's attention.

'Dunno,' Lenny whispered back.

'Take him down into the cellar. Make

him get back in the deep freeze. He'll do it if you tell him. He trusts you.'

'OK,' said Lenny, keeping his eyes on Clum. 'I've got to go now. I think he's getting restless.'

They went down the stairs, with Lenny leading. He was aware that Miss Butterworth was creeping down too, hovering somewhere in the background. But he couldn't worry about her. He had to concentrate on Clum.

Clum could hardly fit on to the twisty stairway. He hopped after Lenny, hunched over like a giant goblin, leaving slimy trails on the wall. But he wasn't in a rage any more. He was croaking in a peaceful, contented way. He thought he'd lost his friend Harold. Now he'd found him. His simple brain was almost overwhelmed with happiness.

Right until they reached the kitchen, Lenny intended to do what Miss Butterworth said – make Clum climb in the freezer and freeze himself all over again. It seemed like a good plan to him. He certainly didn't have a better one.

But down in the kitchen, something happened that totally changed his mind.

Lenny could see the cellar door. It was open. Easy-peasy to lead Clum down there. Clum would follow Harold anywhere; do anything that Harold told him.

The pile of Sparkle Bars was still on the table. Clum gave a croak of pleasure when he saw them. He reached out a finny hand. And Lenny remembered that Clum loved shiny things.

Lenny wasn't sure why he said it. He just wanted Clum to have something nice before he got frozen again for ever. 'Fetch,' he said, just as Harold would have said. 'Go on, you can have one. Fetch!'

He didn't expect what happened next. It was an awful shock; he just hadn't thought things through at all. Because Clum didn't fetch. But some of the squirming bits of Clum did. The ones that were on the outside, still jostling to find a place.

They detached themselves from Clum's body. They came writhing like worms from his head, his arms, his feet. They looped over to the pile, snatched a Sparkle Bar and went back with it, in five seconds flat. It all happened so fast Lenny couldn't take it in. He saw wriggling, glittering, and Clum was suddenly transformed, like magic, before his eyes.

His grotesque warty face was hidden. His froggy features – his slimy body, his webbed hands and feet – disappeared. As the toffee slugs tucked themselves back into place, with the Sparkle Bars on their backs, they made Clum into a fantastical creature, all clothed in silver.

'Wow!!' breathed Lenny, awestruck by the change. 'You look like a noble knight. In beautiful silver armour!'

Clum's hands had silver gauntlets on. His head was a great silver helmet. Only his golden eyes showed through. He looked heroic, mystical, powerful, as he stood in the Toffee Works kitchen. The Sparkle Bars flashed all over his head and body like a thousand silver mirrors.

'You're a silver knight!' said Lenny again, dazzled by the brilliant figure before him.

But Clum didn't understand. His puzzled eyes peeped through the silver helmet. He didn't know what had happened to him.

'Look,' said Lenny. 'Look at yourself.'

Clum cringed. He croaked in distress. He remembered the last time he'd looked at himself – the hideous creature he'd seen.

'Go on, look,' said Lenny. 'Trust me. Don't be scared.'

He had to take Clum's hand. He could do that, now Clum had silver gauntlets on, covering his sticky fingers. Lenny led Clum to one of Miss Butterworth's huge copper pans. The bottom of it gleamed like a big, round mirror.

Clum looked. He sprang back. 'Kerr-oak!'

'It's OK, it's you!' said Lenny. 'It's really you. You look like a silver giant! A shining knight all in armour! Like something out of a legend!'

Lenny didn't think Clum understood about knights and legends. But he could see Clum was entranced by what he saw. He could see how happy it made him. So Lenny felt happy too. And he knew, from that moment, that he couldn't lead Clum down to the cellar and say, 'Clum, climb in that deep freeze. It's OK. Trust me. Climb in, it won't hurt you.' No, he just couldn't say those words.

'I won't do it,' Lenny decided. 'Harold wouldn't have done it. I'm supposed to be Harold. So I'm not going to do it either.'

'Take Clum down to the cellar,' hissed Miss Butterworth, from behind the kitchen door.

She whispered in case Clum heard her. But she needn't have worried. He was still staring into the copper pan. His own image glittered splendidly back at him. He seemed stunned by the change – from a warty frog into a magnificent prince.

'No,' said Lenny. He shrugged, helplessly. 'I can't. I just can't do it. Look at him. Look how pleased he is with himself!'

'Kerroak!'

Clum turned this way and that, and watched his new body flash like silver fire.

'Don't be soppy,' Miss Butterworth snapped back at Lenny. 'You can't get senti- mental about Toffee Creatures. They're too unpredictable. They're a danger to humans!'

But then she said, 'What are you going

to do with him then? We can't keep him here! He might change his mind and wreck the place. Only Harold can control him and you can't pretend you're Harold for ever!'

'Gosh, no!' agreed Lenny, glancing down at his frock. What would happen when his friends came back? When school started again? It was too awful to think about! 'No, I definitely can't!'

'Well, Clum can't stay here,' said Miss Butterworth, in her most forceful voice.

Clum heard her. His body sparkled like a sunburst as he turned in her direction. He croaked – it sounded more like a growl. His silver-gloved hand shot out –'

Lenny reached up and grasped Clum's hand. 'No, Clum! Don't hurt her. Come with me!' And the mighty silver giant followed him, like a little child.

'Where are you two going?' demanded Miss Butterworth, anxiously. She felt suddenly guilty. She didn't care so much about her own skin. But she was so desperate to save the Toffee Works that she was letting this boy take terrible risks.

'I don't know,' said Lenny truthfully.

'We're going anywhere. Away from the Toffee Works. Away from people. Just anywhere.'

'No, come back here. I've changed my mind. He doesn't have to go back in the deep freeze –'

But she was too late. Lenny had already led Clum through the Toffee Museum and outside, on to the dark streets.

Chapter Nine

It was well after midnight. The industrial estate was deserted. The factories were closed. Delivery vans were parked in rows behind high wire fences.

But still Lenny felt conspicuous. He was wearing young Master Harold's Victorian frock and leading a huge Toffee Creature by the hand. A luminous Toffee Creature, silver-plated with Sparkle Bars that glowed in the dark.

He might have thought it was some terrible dream. Only Harold's boots pinched him and reminded him that he was still wide awake.

He could hardly believe it was only yesterday that he'd wandered into the Toffee Museum, just to kill some time.

'Now look at the mess I'm in,' he raved to himself. 'I wish I'd never seen that sign that said "To the Toffee Museum". I wish I'd never heard of Butterworth's stupid toffee!'

He looked up at Clum: 'What are we going to do?' he asked him desperately.

He hadn't realized, but he wasn't talking to Clum in a loud, slow voice any more, as if he was a pct dog, or a little kid or someone stupid. He was talking to him in a normal voice. As if they were friends.

'We're both in big trouble, Clum,' said Lenny.

But Clum didn't answer. He'd caught sight of his own reflection in a moonlit puddle. And he was kneeling down on one knee, gazing at himself, shaking his head with soft croaks of amazement. As if to say, 'Is that fabulous silver creature really me?'

Lenny hated to spoil Clum's happiness. But his mind was a wasps' nest of worries. What would happen when daylight came? They would have to hide somewhere – somewhere far away from people.

'Maybe in the countryside,' thought

Lenny. 'There aren't many people there. Just cows and sheep and fields.'

He had only the vaguest idea where the countryside was. He'd only been to it twice on school trips.

Lenny imagined himself and Clum, two homeless wanderers, moving only at night, hiding out during the day in barns and woods and ditches. And would he have to be Harold for ever? Dressed in these ridiculous Victorian clothes?

'I don't want to be young Master Harold,' thought Lenny frantically, thinking of the gloomy child on the toffee tin. 'I want to be me!'

He felt trapped, at his wits' end. For a moment, the responsibility of looking after Clum was too much to bear.

'Run away!' a little voice in his head urged him. 'Go home to bed. Forget about Clum. He's not your problem.'

It would be the sensible thing to do.

But then Clum got up awkwardly from the pavement. He put a silver-gauntleted hand in Lenny's. He was ready to go. And Lenny knew that he couldn't abandon him.

How would Clum survive on his own? He was a seven-foot tall Toffee Creature. Yet he was as helpless as Lenny's newborn baby sister.

He needed protection. Or he'd end up hurting people. He'd get caught. They'd put him in a cage. He'd be prodded and stared at like some kind of freak! They might even experiment on him in a laboratory!

That idea shocked him so much that Lenny said urgently, 'Come on, Clum! We've got to keep moving.'

What else was there to do? But what would happen when morning came? When Mum looked in his bedroom and found his bed empty?

Lenny groaned hopelessly. He rocked his poor, aching head in his hands: 'I'm in *so much* trouble!'

But then he felt a light touch on his shoulder. He looked up. It was Clum, gazing down at him. His golden-flecked eyes were full of concern.

'Kerroak?'

That meant, 'What's the matter, Harold? What's wrong?' Lenny was getting good at croak language now. He knew what Clum meant, almost every time.

He heard himself saying, 'It's all right, Clum, don't worry. Everything's going to be all right.'

They wandered down the empty roads of the industrial estate. It was like a maze – it seemed to go on for miles. There should have been somewhere to shelter – some empty warehouse, an old shed. Some neglected, forgotten place. But everything was behind barbed wire fences, flooded with security lights. There wasn't even a corner to crawl in and hide.

One sign on a fence said, 'Guard Dogs. Beware!'

'Oh no!' thought Lenny, steering Clum in the other direction. He remembered what Clum had done when the mob set their dogs on him.

Too late. A Doberman flung itself at the fence, barking like crazy. Its mouth was a big, red cave full of fangs and white froth.

Clum turned his great silver head. He drew himself up to his full height. He clumped in a glittering rage towards the wire. He raised his massive fist.

'KERROAK!' His mighty croak was like a T-Rex's roar.

The Doberman took one look at him. 'Yip, yip, yip, yip, yip!' It yelped away, cringing, and hid in the shadows.

'Come on, Clum,' said Lenny, dragging at his silver arm.

There were dangers everywhere.

Lenny didn't see him until they got up close – but there was a man, sleeping rough, curled up on a bench. Clum loomed over him, threateningly. He didn't trust people any more. Except of course, for young Master Harold.

'No!' Lenny yelled at Clum. 'Leave him alone. He won't hurt you!'

Lenny's shout woke the man. He stared up at Clum with bleary eyes. He stared at Lenny in his Scottish cap and lacy frock. For a second he looked startled. Then he told himself, in a sleepy voice, 'I don't believe this, I'm dreaming.' He folded an arm round his head and went back to sleep.

'Phew!' thought Lenny. 'That was close!'

Was nowhere safe for Clum? Desperately, Lenny tried to think of safe places. Could he smuggle Clum up to his bedroom? He wouldn't leave a mess, not now his sticky skin was topped with a smooth, silvery skin of Sparkle Bars.

'No,' thought Lenny. 'Where could I hide him? My mum pokes her nose everywhere, even under the bed.'

Lenny imagined himself, dressed as Harold, introducing Clum to his mum: 'Hi, Mum, this is my new friend Clum! He's a Toffee Creature! He's been deep frozen since 1887!'

'No, no, no, no!' thought Lenny, violently shaking his head. 'It'll never work! Besides, I can't take him home. I can't take him anywhere around people, can I? He's too dangerous.'

So he could never take Clum to school. That was absolutely out of the question. It was a tempting thought, though. Clum would be great protection. None of the bad boys would lay a finger on Lenny while Clum was his bodyguard.

'Mind you,' thought Lenny. 'I'd need Clum to protect me if I had to walk into school dressed like Harold!'

In spite of all his worries, Lenny laughed. Clum copied the sound, making a croaking laugh of his own.

Lenny looked up at Clum. Clum was happy. Happy to be walking with Harold, happy with his new silver body. Happy that no one was yelling at him or chasing him with dogs –

But there was a faint grey light in the East. The long night was nearly over. Soon the early shift would arrive at the factories. Soon this place would be bustling with people.

'And then what on earth are we going to do?' thought Lenny. He still didn't have any answers.

A cold wind was coming up with the dawn. Suddenly, there seemed to be lots of litter blowing around. Lenny and Clum walked past the last factory. Into a moonscape of growling yellow monsters.

It was a landfill site, on the edge of the industrial estate. The floodlights were still on – they'd been working through the night. Yellow JCBs were grinding around in the mud. They had long praying-mantis arms which were jerking up and down.

Clum peered through the wire, astonished. Lenny tried to guess what was going on in his head.

'It's all right, Clum,' he soothed him. 'They won't hurt you. They're just machines. All right? They're just dumper trucks and JCBs and diggers and things. Look, they're tipping rubbish into that great big hole, then making it flat. Come on,' he tugged Clum's arm. 'We've got to get going. It's getting light.'

Clum turned, obediently, to follow. A Sparkle Bar on his shoulder had come unstuck. You could see his real body underneath, warty and sticky-brown. The Sparkle Bar flapped up and down like a loose epaulette. Suddenly, a gust of wind caught it, snatched it into the air, then whisked it off over the wire.

Clum reached after it. He loved shiny things. His arm stretched out like putty, trying to catch it. But being deep frozen, tapped into chunks, then thawed out and re-assembled hadn't improved his co-ordination. He had always been clumsy. Now he was clumsier than ever. So, of course, he missed the Sparkle Bar completely.

But that didn't stop him. It was as if all the toffee slugs that had rushed to the tower room to re-make him were whispering to him: 'Fetch, fetch, fetch!' He just had to obey.

The bar winged its way on the wind, like a sparkling butterfly. It was flying into the heart of the landfill site. Soon it was lost in the dust and the whirling litter. But Clum hadn't lost it. He could sniff it out, even among the stinking garbage.

Lenny watched in horror as Clum lumbered after the Sparkle Bar. He didn't hop gracefully over the wire. He battered it down, like a silver tank.

'No!' yelled Lenny. 'No, Clum! Don't fetch! Don't! Don't!'

But his cry only made it worse. For 'Don't' was drowned out by the snarling landfill machines.

Clum clambered eagerly over the buckled wire. His eyes were bright with purpose. Harold wanted the glittery thing. He had said, 'Fetch!' Nothing would stop Clum now. Nothing. He would do anything to please Harold. Harold was more important to him than anything else in the world.

Even more important than his beautiful silver body. As he climbed over the spiky wire, some of the Sparkle Bars were hooked, like silver fish.

But Clum didn't even notice. He was standing tall, not hunched in his usual froggy crouch. He strode away across the muddy moonscape. He strode into the dust and noise.

A thought flashed through Lenny's mind. 'He looks like a spaceman. In a silver spacesuit.'

Then he had no time for any more thinking. He was too busy chasing Clum. As he scrambled after him, bits of Harold's clothes, shreds of tartan and ripped-off lace, were left dangling on the wire, along with the Sparkle Bars.

The wind was gusting even more

strongly. Lenny staggered, coughing, through a storm of dust and whirling litter. Somewhere, faintly, he could hear machines growling. But his eyes were red and weepy from flying grit. They were stinging like mad; he couldn't see where he was going. He could be going round in circles.

'Clum, Clum, come back! It's dangerous!'

But Clum was unstoppable. Wherever he was, he was on the trail of the Sparkle Bar. He wouldn't give up until he had fetched it for Harold.

'Clum!'

Lenny tripped over a rock, crashed to his knees. The dust storm raged on over his head, making the world seem dark even though the site was lit up like a Christmas tree. Somewhere a hooter was wailing.

His voice was desperate now. 'Clum, can you hear me?'

He listened hard for an answer: 'Ker-roak!' But no answer came.

In fact, there was no sound at all. The machines had stopped working. The men had gone away for a tea break.

Cautiously Lenny raised his head. The

dust clouds had thinned out a bit. They'd switched off the floodlights. He could see the grey dawn sky.

'Clum!'

Still crawling, he groped his way over the ploughed-up mud.

He put out his hand. It touched – empty air.

'Don't move!' his brain shrieked. He was on the edge of a pit, staring right into it! It wasn't just a pit, more like a yawning chasm. You could fit a football stadium in there! And he'd almost tumbled straight in! Silent JCBs were all around him, like sculptures, left just how they'd been when the hooter sounded.

'Phoooar!' gasped Lenny. The stench was choking. It was the rank bonfire smell of lots of rubbish, all squashed up and warm and rotting away underground.

Then Lenny's stinging eyes caught sight of something.

'Oh no!'

Sticking up from the rubbish, right in the centre of the pit, was a silver gauntlet. It glittered like a diamond in the first rays of the rising sun. And held in it, triumphantly, was a Sparkle Bar.

'Clum! Come to Harold! Come on, Clum!'

But the hand sank. The rubbish closed over it like the waves of the sea.

Then, behind Lenny, an engine spluttered into life. A JCB jerked forward. The driver, high up in the cab, couldn't see him. The catcrpillar tracks almost crushed him! Lenny had to dive out of the way.

A shocked voice yelled, 'Hey you! What do you think you're doing! Do you want to get yourself killed, you stupid little –'

But Lenny was already running, running back through the dust to the hole in the fence where Clum had smashed his way through.

He couldn't stay here. There were shouts, running men in yellow hard hats. They were looking for him.

But he hung on to the fence, for as long as he dared. Enough time to see them tipping soil and great boulders into the pit. Avalanches of boulders, dumper truck after dumper truck. Then the big JCBs grinding around on top, making it all flat. Until Clum was buried under tons of rocks and rubbish and there seemed no hope of escape at all.

Chapter Ten

Lenny didn't want to go back home via the Toffee Works. He never wanted to see the place again. But he had to go there, one last time, to get his bike and his trainers and woolly hat.

He hobbled back through the industrial estate. He thought, 'These boots are killing me!'

And then the sad truth really hit him. 'I can take them off,' he thought.

He didn't need them any more. He didn't have to pretend to be Harold. Not now Clum was dead.

He took off the boots and the lacy frock and the tartan cap. The boots were scuffed, the frock and cap in grimy tatters. But he carried the rags carefully, as if they were precious things.

Being Harold had given him a great gift. The gift of being the only human being that Clum loved and trusted. Lenny would have been Harold all over again. He would *even* have worn those silly fancy-dress clothes, made himself look like a prat, if only it had brought Clum back to life again.

'Just when I was getting to know him,' thought Lenny bitterly. 'Just when I was getting to understand croak language!'

For Lenny was convinced that Clum was dead. Nothing could survive being crushed under rocks and then flattened by JCBs.

He walked in his bare feet to the Toffee Works.

Miss Butterworth sprang out at him as soon as he showed his face in the kitchen. She saw his drooping shoulders. She saw him carrying Harold's clothes. Her shrewd lime-drop eyes instantly summed up the situation.

'What happened to Clum?' she asked Lenny.

'He was fetching a Sparkle Bar,'

mumbled Lenny. 'He was really happy! I couldn't stop him. He fell into this great big landfill site. The one just past the pet food factory —'

'Is he dead?' interrupted Miss Butterworth, suspiciously.

''Course he's dead!' exploded Lenny, furious with rage and grief. 'What do you expect him to be? He's under tons of rock! There's those massive machines driving about on top of him!'

'I only asked,' said Miss Butterworth hastily. She wasn't used to comforting people. And, personally, she thought Clum was better off out of the way. It was a big load off her mind. But she saw how upset Lenny was. She searched around in her brain for some way of making him feel better.

'You saved my Toffee Works!' she said to him. 'It would have been a pile of rubble but for you. You know, I had a premonition when you came in wheeling that bike. I said to myself, 'Araminta, that boy has toffee in his blood or I'm not a Butterworth! He will be our guardian angel!'

'I don't want to be an angel!' protested Lenny, bitterly. 'I don't want anything else to do with toffee! And I don't think saving this dump is any big deal! Clum had the right idea! It should be turned into a heap of bricks. It should be totally demolished!'

'Oh dear,' thought Miss Butterworth to herself. 'That didn't work very well.'

'I liked Clum!' Lenny burst out, his lower lip trembling. 'I could've taught him things! He would've been all right!'

'No, he wouldn't!' contradicted Miss Butterworth sharply. She made her voice gentler. 'You know he wouldn't.'

Lenny said nothing.

'Here's your shoes by the way,' she said. 'I brought them down from the tower room.'

Lenny took them and silently put them on.

'Here's your woolly hat.'

Lenny put it on and, in return, he laid Harold's clothes and boots, or what was left of them, on the table by the twisted candy sticks.

He noticed that there was a Sparkle Bar on the floor. The toffee slugs must have missed it. But he didn't pick it up. He would never eat a Sparkle Bar ever again. It would bring back too many memories.

Lenny knew, in his heart, that Miss Butterworth was absolutely right about Clum. He was a primitive Toffee Creature. How could he fit into the modern world? Except as a freak in a cage.

'You said he was happy,' said Miss Butterworth. 'You made him happy. I think you should be very proud about that.'

But Lenny didn't want to talk about it. He didn't want to admit she was right. His feelings of loss were still too raw. He grabbed his bike and rushed out of the Toffee Works without even saying goodbye.

Miss Butterworth gazed after him. She felt she had handled things badly.

'You made a right mess of that,' she scolded herself. 'That boy had potential! You could have taught him everything you know. How to throw toffee. How to make toffee baskets. Even how to make toffee swans –'

Lenny was really lucky when he got home. His mum and dad were up, but they

144

were busy with the baby. So he was able to creep upstairs, leap back into bed and pull the duvet right over his head, without anyone even noticing he'd been gone.

Chapter Eleven

Lenny's friends came back from holiday. They all brought him great presents. Neil brought him a designer T-shirt. He said, as he handed it over: ''Course, it's only a fake.'

Lenny said, 'I don't care! I like it better than the real thing!'

Weeks and weeks passed. His baby sister stopped being so much of a pain. She even started to smile at him. Mum let him pick her up and play with her whenever he liked.

Gradually his memories of Clum grew less painful. Sometimes he didn't think about him for days at a time.

He didn't tell his friends what had happened – they wouldn't have believed him.

They might have believed the bit about the Toffee Creature. But they *definitely* wouldn't believe that he'd walked round the streets in a Victorian boy's lacy frock. They'd think he'd gone crazy. They'd say: 'Prove it!' And he had nothing to prove it, nothing at all. Sometimes, even to him, it seemed like a really weird dream. He thought, 'Did that really happen?'

He asked himself that again, when in the Christmas holidays, he found himself cycling round the industrial estate. He was waiting for Neil. But Neil was late as usual. He was probably watching the cartoons on telly.

Lenny rode about. He had to, to keep warm. It was a freezing cold day, with a sprinkling of snow on the ground.

Suddenly, he found himself at the end of that alley. The one full of wheelie bins and rubbish. He hadn't been to this part of the industrial estate since that terrible day when Clum had got buried in the landfill site.

But strangely, he had had a dream last night about Miss Butterworth. In the dream he had seen her toffee throwing. She wasn't in a kitchen. She was on top of a high hill throwing toffee, making glorious, golden arcs in the sky! And he had heard himself say, in the dream, 'I want to do that!'

He had promised himself that he wouldn't go near the Toffee Works. His life was back to normal now; he just wanted to forget all about it. But, as he hesitated at the end of the alley, he made a bargain with himself: 'I'll just ride past, there, OK? I won't go in. I'll just ride past.'

So he did. In fact, he'd got right to the other end of the alley before he thought, 'Where is it? I can't have missed it!'

He rode back again, slowly this time. Warehouse, scrap yard, another warehouse, some wheelie bins. That's where it had been – there. But there was just a gap, clean as a missing tooth. The Toffee Works had gone, been sucked into space, spirited off the face of the earth!

Not even one crumbling yellow brick remained, to show it had ever existed.

Had it ever existed? Was it all just a dream? Lenny's stomach gave a sick lurch, like it does when you miss your step on the stairs. He felt dizzy, bewildered. What was going on?

'I'm going round the bend!' he thought. 'I can't really have imagined it, can I? Miss Butterworth and Harold and Clum. I couldn't have made them up! They're too weird! No one could make *them* up!'

Still dazed, he got on his bike. He hardly noticed where he was pedalling. Until he stopped to blow on his icy, blue hands to warm them up. And found that he'd cycled right past the petfood factory and was staring at the landfill site.

He couldn't believe his eyes. For there, staring into the site, hanging on to the wire, was Miss Butterworth. At first, he thought he'd make a mistake.

'No,' he thought, 'it can't be her.'

Then he cycled closer. She was muffled up in a scarf and hat and mittens. But he recognized those green rubber boots, those even greener lime-drop eyes. It was her all right.

'Miss Butterworth! Miss Butterworth! It's me, Lenny! What you doing here?'

To his surprise, he was really pleased to see her.

'I'm not going round the bend after all,' he thought, relieved. 'It must have really happened!'

And Miss Butterworth's first words to him were the final proof.

'Is this the place where poor old Clum got buried?'

'Yes,' said Lenny.

He too stared through the wire. The machines weren't working today. The ground was frozen solid. It was like iron.

'I thought,' said Miss Butterworth, 'that I'd take a little trip here, to see for myself.'

'A little trip,' said Lenny amazed. 'I thought you never went anywhere!'

'Oh, all that's changed,' shrugged Miss Butterworth. 'I'm quite a gad-about now. I meet more people than you can shake a stick at! Crowds and crowds of people come to the Toffee Works. Business is really booming!'

Lenny felt his head spinning. Every time he thought things were straightened out, that life was back to normal, something happened to scramble his brain again.

'Wait a minute!' he begged. 'Just wait a minute! I've been to the Toffee Works. I was there just now. And there's nothing there! There's a big hole where it was. I mean, don't tell me it's invisible or something! That's what you're going to tell me, aren't you?' said Lenny rather hysterically. 'It's an invisible Toffee Works now, isn't it?'

'Tut, tut,' said Miss Butterworth, raising her eyebrows. 'Young man, where do you get your ideas from? Of course it's not invisible. That would be silly! They've just moved it, that's all. Lock, stock and barrel. They've moved it into the Victorian street at the Heritage Museum!'

'What,' said Lenny, still confused. 'They moved everything! Even the humbug machine?'

'Oh yes,' said Miss Butterworth. 'They wanted all the old machines. They were very particular about that. They got the humbug machine out with a crane, after they took off the glass dome. It was quite a sight, you should have been there! They numbered every brick and put them back just as before. The Toffee Works is exactly the same, except it's at a museum.'

'Is the tower room still there?'

'Of course,' said Miss Butterworth. 'Didn't you see it in the newspapers? There were photos!'

'I don't read our paper,' said Lenny. 'Except for the television page and the funnies. What about Harold's clothes and his horse? What about his picture on the toffee tin? They haven't thrown them away, have they?'

'Over my dead body!' said Miss Butterworth, in a highly indignant voice. 'I wouldn't let them do that! Young Harold is part of our toffee history. A very important part. He will never be forgotten! Not while I'm alive he won't!'

'Good,' said Lenny. He would never forget Harold either – that pasty-faced, serious child on the toffee tin. How could he, when he had actually *been* Harold? It wasn't for long. But those hours with Clum the Toffee Creature had been the most magical, the most hair-raising, the most incredible time of his whole life.

'We were even on local radio. On the *Tea-time Show*!' Miss Butterworth was telling him excitedly. 'That day you rode off on your bike, that very day, some smart young men in suits from the Council came round. They said, "Miss Butterworth, we want to preserve your Toffee Works. It is part of our heritage." And it's all in working order too!'

'You mean, you can still make toffee?' asked Lenny.

'Every day!' said Miss Butterworth. 'It's wonderful! It's like old times! I'm making all the old-fashioned sweets: humbugs, pear drops, sour apples, acid drops, sugar sticks, cinder toffee. They're really popular – with children, with old folk, with everyone! I can hardly keep up with the demand. In fact,' she said, looking at Lenny shrewdly. 'I could really do with some help. Not from just any-one, of course. I'm very choosy. It's got to be someone with a feeling for toffee. Someone who's got toffee in their blood.'

'Hummmm,' said Lenny, shuffling his

feet about. Quickly, he changed the subject. 'Anyway,' he asked her, 'what are you doing here? What *exactly*?'

He didn't think she was making a sentimental journey to see where Clum was buried. Hadn't she said: *You can't be sentimental about Toffee Creatures*?

Miss Butterworth opened her mouth to tell him. Then she had second thoughts. 'Actually,' she said, 'perhaps I should get a grip.' She stared out over the frozen landfill site. Her thoughts seemed far, far away. 'I'm just a silly old woman,' she said. 'There's nothing to be afraid of.'

Suddenly, a terrible knowledge flooded Lenny's brain. He found he could read her mind, like he could read Clum's. It must be something they all had in common . . .'

'You don't think he's dead, do you?' he challenged her. 'Do you?'

'We-e-e-e-l-ll,' admitted Miss Butterworth, chewing thoughtfully on one of her furry mittens. 'It had occurred to me. I thought he was dead once before. I was sure of it. And I was wrong then, wasn't I?'

'He is dead,' insisted Lenny, in a panicky voice. ''Course he is! Look, he's under the ground. Under tons of mud and rock! Nothing could survive that!'

'On the other hand,' said Miss Butterworth, 'toffee is an amazing material. It's very, very adaptable. It's practically indestructible. Have you ever tried to get toffee out of your hair, for example?'

Lenny went wild. He stamped his feet like a toddler. 'This is a ridiculous conversation!' he roared. 'And I'm not going to listen to it any more! He's dead, he's not coming back! I've just got used to the idea. I don't want my mind all messed up again!'

Would he want Clum to come back to life? Lenny just didn't know. In some ways he would. He'd got really fond of Clum, in the short time he'd known him. But in other ways it would be a major, major headache. Lenny couldn't even begin to think about all the problems involved. They were just too massively mind-boggling.

'I – don't – want – to – think – about – it!' he bellowed, his breath coming out in frosty clouds.

'All right, all right,' soothed Miss Butterworth. 'Don't get your knickers in a twist. Don't take any notice of me. I'm a dozy old bat. I get these silly ideas in my head –'

'I'm going now,' said Lenny abruptly. He wanted to get away from the frozen wastes of the landfill site. It looked as cold and grim as the Arctic out there.

Miss Butterworth fixed him with her gimlet eyes. 'So – are you coming to the Heritage Museum then? I'll pay you, of course. It'll be a nice little earner. A bit of pocket money for you.'

'What?' said Lenny brightening up. 'As toffee consultant, like we said?'

'Oh no,' said Miss Butterworth. 'Not as a toffee consultant. I don't need one of those now. Not with Butterworth's toffee being so popular. More popular than those darn Sparkle Bars, I'll be bound! No, what I need now is a hands-on type of person. A toffee expert who knows toffee inside out! I could train you up,' she told him, coolly. 'You'd be very good at it.'

Despite himself, Lenny was flattered. 'A

toffee expert!' he murmured. He liked the sound of that.

'I'm not all that brilliant at anything really,' he thought. It would be nice to have something he could shine at. And toffee throwing still made his heart leap. He wanted to have a go at it. He really did. He secretly dreamed of spinning life-size toffee swans, like Granny Wang's granny. Although he daren't tell that dream to Miss Butterworth. She might say, 'Toffee swans? I've never heard of such nonsense!'

But Lenny's mind was tugged in two directions. Part of him said, 'Get on your bike. Ride away! Far away!'

He had serious doubts about getting involved with toffee. Look what a mess he'd got into before. Just by wandering into a Toffee Works!

'So,' said Miss Butterworth, casually. 'I'll see you then, shall I? At the Heritage Museum, by the Civic Centre?'

Lenny mumbled something. It could have been a yes or a no. Then he got on his bike and cycled away. More snow was drifting down. It made his black woolly hat sparkle.

It crunched like cornflakes under his bike wheels.

Miss Butterworth gazed after him with her far-seeing eyes. Then she turned and stared out over the snowy landfill site. Nothing moved out there. It was silent and cold as the grave.

Miss Butterworth shivered.

'I wonder,' she said to herself. 'I wonder.'

Epilogue

'More humbugs!' cried Miss Butter-worth. 'More humbugs!'

Lenny adjusted a dial on the monster machine. The big paddles whacked even faster. More stripy humbugs came joggling along the conveyor belt.

Lenny had learned to work the humbug machine. He had learned all sorts of things since he started working Saturdays for Miss Butterworth.

He'd had a big struggle in his mind. Should he go? Should he stay away? But one Saturday morning it was raining and he was fed up and broke and there was nothing on telly and none of his mates was coming out. And suddenly the decision seemed really easy.

'About time,' Miss Butterworth had said to him, when he finally turned up at the Toffee Works in the Heritage Museum. 'I could do with some help.' She didn't seem at all surprised to see him.

The Toffee Works looked a bit different. It was in a cobbled Victorian street now, with a shop selling penny-farthing bicycles on one side and a clock maker's on the other. And the old Toffee Museum – the one Lenny had wandered into – wasn't there any more. It had been turned into a little shop, to sell Butterworth's sweets and toffee to the crowds of visitors who wanted to buy them.

But some things hadn't changed. Harold's clothes were still shut away upstairs in the cupboard in the tower room. Along with his toy horse and the toffee tin with his picture on it.

'I washed his frock and Scottish cap,' Miss Butterworth told Lenny, 'And patched them up and they look almost as good as new!'

Today they were run off their feet. It was the first day of spring and the warm weather had brought lots of visitors. All of them seemed to want a little paper cone filled with sugar twists, raspberry drops or banana-flavoured toffee fudge.

BOING, BOING!

'Time for toffee-throwing!' said Miss Butterworth briskly, glancing at the Toffee Works clock.

This was Lenny's favourite time of day. Visitors were already crowding at the kitchen door waiting for the show to begin. The toffee throwing was a big attraction. People came from miles around to see it.

'To you!' cried Miss Butterworth, when they'd both greased their hands. She lobbed a lump of hot toffee at him. After years of being a hermit it was amazing how she'd blossomed.

'She shows off nearly as much as I do!' thought Lenny, fondly.

Miss Butterworth didn't need the hook in the wall any more. She had Lenny instead. She and Lenny worked as a team, twirling the toffee like skipping ropes between them.

It had taken Lenny ages to learn. At first, he'd burned his hands, he hadn't worked fast enough. He'd fumbled and dropped the toffee. He'd snapped the ropes. Lots of times, he'd nearly cried with frustration. But he hadn't given up.

And now he was a star. He could juggle those ropes like an old hand. He and Miss Butterworth, working together, fast as lightning, made their audience gasp and go 'Ahhh!' as if they were watching a fireworks display.

It was a tricky toffee throwing. They were making peppermint twists with two green peppermint ropes and two plain toffee ones.

Soon the kitchen was whirling with rainbows in glittering gold and green.

'Ahhh!' went the audience, their eyes rolling like marbles as they tried to follow the loops around.

The loops got bigger and floppier as the toffee stretched. Lenny and Miss Butterworth moved further apart until their backs were against the kitchen walls and there was no more space left to work in. Soon those toffee ropes would stick to the ceiling! They were going to break any second!

'Now!' cried Miss Butterworth. It was

perfect timing. She stood stock still, holding four toffee ropes . . .

Lenny's hands were a blur, like fluttering wings. Criss, cross, criss, cross, he plaited away like fury. Until they were holding between them one long peppermint twist that stretched right across the kitchen.

'Phew!' thought Lenny. That was close. The toffee had almost got the better of them. You could never tell with toffee. It seemed to have moods, like a living creature. Sometimes you could tame it. Sometimes it had a will of its own.

The audience clapped, they cheered. 'Bravo!' It was a dazzling display. Lenny bowed, gave a modest grin.

'Can we buy some of that!' yelled some kid in a bright yellow jacket, pushing his way into the kitchen.

'Not yet!' snapped Miss Butterworth as she chopped the stick into handy lengths. 'Can't you see it isn't set yet? And I don't allow boys in here, they're unhygienic!'

'What about him?' said the kid, pointing accusingly at Lenny. 'He's a boy, isn't he?'

'He's different,' declared Miss Butterworth

as if it should be obvious to anyone. 'He belongs in here.'

The kid retreated, looking baffled. Lenny sighed. He was always telling Miss Butterworth to be nicer to children. But she was still as prickly as ever. Unless, of course, she suspected you'd got toffee in your blood.

'A good bit of toffee throwing that,' admitted Miss Butterworth. 'Good team work.'

Lenny smiled. He was encouraged. There was something he'd been meaning to tell her. And he thought now might be the right time.

'My Granny Wang's granny,' he began, 'back in China – she was a famous toffee maker.'

'I knew it! I knew it!' said Miss Butterworth. 'I knew you came from a toffee family. I've even heard of the Wangs! Everyone who knows about toffee history knows about the famous Wang family!'

'My mum told me,' said Lenny, 'that Granny Wang's granny used to spin toffee somehow. And she used to make toffee swans. Life-size toffee swans –'

Lenny waited for Miss Butterworth to say, 'Toffee swans! What would anyone want with a toffee swan?'

But she didn't. To his amazement she said, 'I used to do swans.'

'Honest?'

'Yes, you spin the toffee in long threads from a broom handle. Then you sort of shape it into a swan. I'm a bit rusty, mind. I haven't done swans for fifty years or more. But I can show you how to do it, if you like.'

'Please!' said Lenny, thrilled to bits. 'And when I get good at it, I'm going to take one round to Granny Wang.'

'You do that,' said Miss Butterworth. 'You could even bring her round here. It would be an honour to meet someone like her. From such a distinguished toffee family . . .'

While Lenny and Miss Butterworth chatted happily about toffee swan making, something was happening out on the landfill site.

It had been a hard winter. But for days now a hazy, yellow sun had been thawing the frozen mud. There were even some green shoots of grass poking through.

Underground the rubbish was getting active, warming up, shifting around, chemicals trickling into other chemicals, combining, reacting, cascading, making new compounds.

The toffee was warming up too. It had been squished and squelched into a thousand cracks and crevices. But gradually, very gradually, it joined the chemical flow. It began to creep back into one great toffee lump, bringing along any Sparkle Bars it happened to meet on the way.

The spring flowers were out before there were any signs above ground. It was Sunday. The workmen had the day off, the JCBs were silent. So, unseen by anyone, there was a little commotion in the middle of the landfill site. As if a mole was busy throwing up heaps of earth.

What looked like a big silver crocus pushed its way through the soil. But it wasn't a crocus. It was a silver-gauntleted hand – rather tatty and tarnished but still shining. For a few seconds the hand stayed perfectly still. It flashed like silver fire in the sunshine.

Then the fingers began to wriggle.

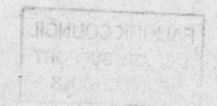

Choosing a brilliant book
can be a tricky business...
but not any more

www.puffin.co.uk

The best selection of books at your fingertips

So get clicking!

Searching the site is easy – you'll find
what you're looking for at the click of a mouse,
from great authors to brilliant books and more!

Read more in Puffin

For complete information about books available from Puffin – and Penguin – and how to order them, contact us at the appropriate address below. Please note that for copyright reasons the selection of books varies from country to country.

www.puffin.co.uk

In the United Kingdom: Please write to Dept EP, Penguin Books Ltd, Bath Road, Harmondsworth, West Drayton, Middlesex UB7 0DA

In the United States: Please write to Penguin Putnam Inc., P.O. Box 12289, Dept B, Newark, New Jersey 07101–5289 or call 1–800–788–6262

In Canada: Please write to Penguin Books Canada Ltd, 10 Alcorn Avenue, Suite 300, Toronto, Ontario M4V 3B2

In Australia: Please write to Penguin Books Australia Ltd, P.O. Box 257, Ringwood, Victoria 3134

In New Zealand: Please write to Penguin Books (NZ) Ltd, Private Bag 102902, North Shore Mail Centre, Auckland 10

In India: Please write to Penguin Books India Pvt Ltd, 11 Panscheel Shopping Centre, Panscheel Park, New Delhi 110 017

In the Netherlands: Please write to Penguin Books Netherlands bv, Postbus 3507, NL–1001 AH Amsterdam

In Germany: Please write to Penguin Books Deutschland GmbH, Metzlerstrasse 26, 60594 Frankfurt am Main

In Spain: Please write to Penguin Books S. A., Bravo Murillo 19, 1° B, 28015 Madrid

In Italy: Please write to Penguin Italia s.r.l., Via Felice Casati 20, I–20124 Milano

In France: Please write to Penguin France S. A., 17 rue Lejeune, F–31000 Toulouse

In Japan: Please write to Penguin Books Japan, Ishikiribashi Building, 2–5–4, Suido, Bunkyo-ku, Tokyo 112

In South Africa: Please write to Longman Penguin Southern Africa (Pty) Ltd, Private Bag X08, Bertsham 2013